VALENTINE'S COWBOY RESCUE

Cowboys of Wildcat Creek, Book One

BARBARA MCMAHON

Valentine's Cowboy Rescue
Copyright © 2022 Barbara McMahon
All Rights Reserved

1

Jenny stopped the jeep a few feet from the cabin. The three wooden steps leading up to the porch were already covered in several inches of snow as was everything else in sight.

"We made it," she said to the large German Shepherd dog sitting attentively beside her.

Val whined to get out. He'd patiently sat through the trying drive from town without a whimper, skids and all, but now that they were home, he was excited to get out and play in the snow.

"Okay, hold on. I'll let you out in a second."

She smiled at her companion and opened her door—quickly sliding out. He followed a half second later. She'd learned early on when she first got him that he always wanted out of a car and if she didn't move fast enough, he'd sail right over her once the door was open.

He ran in the snow and barked in delight. Stopping to roll in the white stuff, he stood again, looking like a ghost.

She laughed. She loved that dog. He brought her so much joy. More than what she expected when they were first paired up.

Taking a deep breath of the frigid air she raised her gaze

to the tree tops, some branches already bending slightly with the weight of the snow. The cold, crisp air felt good. And so different from the hot, dusty air of Afghanistan. Gazing around, she relished the tall evergreens, the clearing in which her small cabin sat. Silence seemed even more muted with the snow. Except for the dog running around, she could almost hear the snowflakes landing.

She loved being home. She'd been lucky to rent the cabin when she returned to Wildcat Creek. It suited her perfectly and felt like home from the first day.

"I wish you could help me unload," she called as she pulled four bags of groceries from the back seat.

The weather forecast had predicted a record snowfall when this blizzard moved in and she'd stocked up for several weeks. She could cocoon herself in the cabin, self sufficient if the predicted snowfall arrived.

It was falling so thick she could hardly see more than a few dozen yards in front of her.

Jenny trudged carefully up the steps to the porch. The overhang sheltered most of it from the snow. Putting down a couple of bags, she unlocked the door. The cabin was toasty warm. Quickly carrying the bags to the kitchen, she turned to bring in another load.

The large stack of firewood, protected on the porch, would last for days. The major stack of wood for the winter was close enough to the house she could shovel a path to it when the logs on the porch became depleted.

She had a generator if the power went out as it often did this far from town when heavy snow or fallen trees pulled down the lines.

Two more trips and the jeep was empty. Val ran around in the snow, sticking his nose into the white stuff then tossing his head up causing a small arc of snow that drifted in the wind. Jenny laughed again.

"Shall I throw you some snowballs?" she asked. Taking a handful of snow, she packed it into a ball and then threw it. The dog ran after it, then stopped—puzzled. He sniffed around, sticking his nose into the snow, looking for the ball.

Laughing again, Jenny played the game with him for several minutes. She tossed some gently and he'd jump to catch them mid-air, only to bite down on them and sending snow cascading from his mouth.

Finally she called a halt.

"Come on, let's go inside. The snow's getting deeper and it's cold and I still have to put the groceries away."

Val trotted over and once on the porch shook off the accumulation of snow transforming himself from white to black.

"Glad we have this porch or you'd be making a bigger mess inside," she said, opening the door to let the dog in.

By the time Jenny finished putting the groceries away, she was ready for lunch. At one point that morning she'd debated staying in town to treat herself to lunch from the café, but when the snow began falling heavily she knew she'd better get home before the roads became impassable.

A loud crack came from outside, then two muffled thumps.

Jenny froze for a split second, then dropped to all fours and scurried beneath the dining room table, her mind taking her back to the ambush in Afghanistan. She couldn't move, she could scarcely breath. Visions of that attack flooded her mind. Adrenalin surged, her heart pounded, her vision was obscured. She heard the echo of the mortar rounds. Felt the incessant heat. Heard the cries of the wounded, the rounds of gunfire. She drew herself into a ball, trying to hide where there was no hiding. Trying to be safe until she could move again.

Val leaned against her, sticking his face in front of hers, licking her cheek. He whimpered, pushing against her and licking her face over and over.

Slowly the images and sounds faded. She reached for her service dog and buried her face in his thick fur hugging him tight. Taking a deep breath, she willed her mind to come back to the present. Wished her racing heart would slow down. Wished she could forget.

The dog remained in position, leaning against her slightly, not moving until she did. Slowly her breathing returned to normal. Slowly she opened her eyes and saw the furnishings in the cabin she rented.

She wasn't in Afghanistan. She was in Wyoming.

She wasn't in the Army any more. She was home.

Safe at home.

"Stupid, huh," she said into his fur, still clinging to her dog as the adrenalin slowly dissipated. "A tree limb probably broke dumping snow."

She hated this. The psychiatrist at the VA hospital had told her the attacks would most likely fade over time–lots of time. Sudden loud noises seem to trigger events. Or sensory overload if she was in a crowded noisy place. Or stress. Or nothing at all.

Jenny reviewed what she was doing to manage the PTSD. To minimize triggers.

She lived alone in a quiet home tucked away in a section of a peaceful forest. Neighbors weren't too far away, but she couldn't hear them when she was outside.

Her trips to town were manageable. Wildcat Creek was a small ranching community—nothing like big cities with constant noise and activity.

Her job as a private duty nurse suited her situation. Fortunately the residents of Wildcat Creek and nearby towns where she might be called to work knew her situation and her service dog was as welcomed as she was.

She sat back on the floor and continued to hold on to Val. He climbed into her lap, his face still studying hers. His hundred pounds was a welcomed weight against her legs.

"You aren't exactly a lap dog," she said as she petted him.

Taking deep breaths, she tried to orient herself. In a moment, she'd get up, fix her lunch, and be fine the rest of the day.

Or she would be when the adrenalin surge subsided.

She hoped.

"If I only had a second's warning, I could prepare," she murmured to Val.

He thumped his tail on the floor, still pinning her legs to the floor, leaning against her slightly, giving the support she needed.

"Okay, I'm good."

He rose and she scooted out from beneath the table. Jenny stood up and then leaned over to hug her dog again.

"Thanks for being here for me," she said.

She ate lunch at the round oak table to one side of the great room gazing out the front window. The storm was fast becoming the predicted blizzard. The snow so thick she could scarcely see it piling up on the jeep.

"I know you love playing in the snow, but a quiet afternoon inside is in store for us. If it stops snowing tomorrow, we'll play outside," she said to Val.

The dog was curled in front of the fireplace, his gaze on her. He wagged his tail.

Suddenly he rose, ran to the window and looked out, ears up, tail out, his full attention on something outside.

"What is it? A deer? Some old cow that broke through the fence?"

Wild life wasn't uncommon. Even cows sometimes wandered around due to the fact the cabin was actually on a portion of one of the large ranches in the area. Apart from this area of trees that continued upward for several miles, most of the land around Wildcat Creek was rough pasture for the cattle that built the economy in the area.

Val was on alert. He didn't move—ears forward, eyes gazing as if seeing a long distance through the swirling snow. Then he whined, running to the door. Barking, he looked back at her.

"We're not going outside. It's cold, the snow's getting too deep to walk in and I told you we'd play tomorrow."

He nosed the door and barked again. He looked back at her and then barked.

"What is it?" she asked, becoming concerned. He'd never acted this way before.

He barked again, several times, almost as if he was chastising her.

"Okay, okay."

Jenny pulled on her heavy winter coat and flipped the hood over her head.

"Okay, we'll see what's got you all worked up. But if it's a squirrel or something, I'm not going to be happy."

She opened the door and he shot outside like a bullet, running past the jeep and down the driveway.

"Val, come," she called, hurrying after him. Where was that dog going?

The snow was already a foot deep. She hurried after him, slipping now and then.

It took several minutes to catch up with him. He continued to bark and when she rounded a curve in the driveway, she saw him on the road. Not that it was easy to see, the snow blended everywhere. She'd been lucky to find her way back home earlier.

As Jenny approached her barking dog she saw a white pick up truck had gone into the ditch on the other side of the road. Val stood near the driver's door barking furiously.

Jenny hurried to join him. The truck already had a thick coating of snow and due to the angle of incline in the ditch, the side window was coated as well.

She scraped the driver's side window clear and peered inside.

A man sat behind the wheel, his head resting on the back

of the seat, a trickle of blood running down the side of his head.

She pounded on the window. For a moment, nothing happened. Then he opened his eyes, blinked once and turned to stare at her.

Jenny tugged on the door handle and pulled the door open.

"Are you okay?" she asked, leaning in slightly to see him better.

"I've been better."

He looked out the door, then back at the covered windshield.

"I thought I could make it back before the snow got too deep. Guess I figured that wrong."

Jenny straightened, noticing he wore jeans and a shearling jacket over a flannel shirt. Beyond him on the front seat was the ubiquitous cowboy hat.

"Judging from the angle of the truck, I'd say you aren't going to back it out any time soon. And even if you did get it out under its own power, I doubt you'd get five feet down the road. The snow's more than a foot deep already. And you can see how heavy it's coming down."

His hand rubbed his forehead.

Looking closely, she noticed a slight bump.

"Did you hit your head?"

"I think I whacked it on the window when the truck spun and then slammed into the ditch."

"You can't stay here. You'll freeze to death. You'd better come back with me."

He looked around. "Where's your house?"

She pointed across the road to the wide space between the trees. "Down that way."

He looked at her and then at the German Shepherd standing right next to Jenny.

"You're the Army veteran. I heard you lived outside town."

She nodded. "Jenny Schofield. Come on, it's getting colder by the minute. Do you need any help?"

He shook his head slightly, grimaced, and climbed out of the truck. He set his hat on his head, wincing slightly when it touched the abraded area.

"I'm Tucker Mason. Folks call me Tuck."

"And you live in Wildcat Creek?"

"On the Bar 7 Ranch on the other side of town. I'm segundo there."

"Bill Mackay's place?"

He nodded, then winced again. "Yep."

Val danced around.

"Let's go home," she told the big dog.

He turned and led the way back toward the cabin trotting ahead of them, but not too far ahead Jenny couldn't follow.

Tuck walked beside her.

He was tall with that slim physique common to cowboys— wide shoulders, long legs—and of course wearing cowboy boots. Which wouldn't offer much traction in the snow.

He kept pace with her despite the head injury and boots more suited to riding than tramping through snow.

"Does your head hurt?" she asked.

"A bit."

"I'll look at it when we reach home, I'm a nurse."

"Fine."

They walked in silence the rest of the way. Jenny was grateful for Val's leading. The snow was swirling around them so much she might have walked right off the driveway into the trees and been lost. At least there was no wind at the moment.

Her curiosity about the cowboy at her side rose. She didn't know everyone in town, of course, but she did know most. Or heard of them. She didn't think she'd ever heard of Tucker Mason.

She'd been gone for six years and only back a few months. She'd been surprised at how much changed in her absence. As a child growing up in Wildcat Creek, she'd believed nothing changed in a hundred years.

"Are you from around here?" she asked.

How much farther to the cabin? She was cold and felt she'd been walking miles. She kept her hands balled up in her pockets. Once or twice she slid in the uneven ground beneath the snow, but kept on.

"From the Bar 7," he said again.

"Born and raised there?" she asked with some asperity. She wasn't senile, she heard him the first time he'd said it.

"No, born and raised in Texas."

His voice held a hint of Texas drawl.

"How long have you been here in Wyoming?" she asked.

He looked down at her. She met his gaze, knowing hers was full of curiosity. This man she met a few moments ago already intrigued her.

"A while."

She wrinkled her nose and faced forward. Either he was super secretive or just didn't want to open up.

Which raised her curiosity a notch higher.

"Do you know where you're going?" he asked a moment later.

The thick snow made it impossible to see more than a few feet in front of them.

"I'm relying on Val to lead the way," she said. "He'll get us home. My driveway's long. He must have heard your crash though I can't imagine how. The snow muffles everything. He was in an all fired hurry to get out and headed straight for you."

"I appreciate the rescue."

They trudged along in silence for several minutes. Then the snow covered jeep appeared and finally the cabin.

"We're here," she said, following Val up the steps to the porch. After they brushed off most of the snow, she opened the door and led the way inside.

"Man this feels great," Tuck said, removing his hat and holding it in his hand.

She could almost see him soaking up the warmth. She took off her jacket and watched as he assessed her home.

Tuck looked around the cabin, glad for the warmth. It looked like it was one large room with furniture designating the different areas–living, dining. The kitchen opened to the room and had a door leading outside. Three doors on the back wall were closed. Bedrooms and bath were his guess.

"You can hang your coat and hat on the rack," she said,

pointing out the hooks on the wall beside the door. She'd already hung her jacket and was walking toward the back.

He nodded, taking off his jacket. The place was snug and warm. Too bad he'd have to head back out as soon as he could get his truck towed. There was too much work waiting at the ranch to give into a sudden desire to just sit down and soak up the warmth. And if the storm delivered all the snow that was forecast, there'd be even more things to deal with.

"Can I use your phone?" he asked.

"Sure, but let me look at your head first."

That same head that was pounding like a jackhammer. He took a deep breath. Then followed her to the bathroom. He felt the trickle of blood on his face now that the warmth started the flow again.

"I can wash up," he said, peering at his reflection in the mirror. Not too bad. He'd had worse.

"Sit down and I'll wash it and assess the damage," she said in a no-nonsense voice.

"Bossy," he muttered.

"What?"

"I've had worse being tossed from a bull."

"Oh great, a rodeo cowboy."

He couldn't read her expression. Did she like rodeo cowboys or not?

She pulled out a washcloth from the small linen closet and let the sink water run until it was hot.

"Not any more," he said.

"The reason for the move to Wyoming?"

He didn't reply, just shrugged.

He hadn't told anyone why he left Texas. If asked directly, he'd reply he'd been looking for a change. The men at the ranch didn't question him. Even Bill Mackay left it alone after the first casual question during their interview.

Her touch was gentle. He closed his eyes and willed the throbbing to go away. It didn't work. The warm cloth felt good against his cool skin. He could tell she was gently wiping the blood away. A moment later he felt a cool spray. Snapping his eyes open he looked at the spray can of antiseptic.

"I have some aspirin if you have a headache."

"I'll take it."

"You've got a goose egg and the skin seemed to split when you hit the window. I don't think you need stitches."

When she turned back to the sink to rinse out the washcloth, he rose. Sitting here wasn't getting him anywhere.

And being next to a pretty woman wasn't going anywhere either. He and women didn't mix well. He'd learned that lesson the hard way.

"I appreciate the help. Can I use your phone now?"

"Of course."

He'd seen it on the wall near the kitchen cabinets. Dialing the ranch, he wanted to let them know he was on his way.

"Mackay," his boss answered.

"It's Tuck. I was heading back from Coleville trying to beat the storm and my truck slid off the road and into a ditch. I'm still a few miles outside of town. I need to get a tow to get it out and then I'll be on my way."

"It's snowing to beat the band out here," his boss said.

"I know. Here, too."

He rubbed his forehead, hoping to ease the ache.

"Where are you exactly?"

"I'm at Jenny Schofield's place. It's a mile or so past Walt Nelson's ranch. Her dog heard the truck crash I guess. Anyway she and the dog rescued me or I'd be half frozen by now. I'll call for a tow and get on my way. I'll let you know when I'm ready to leave. Depends on when Troy can get out."

"The plows can't keep up with the snowfall. If the storm doesn't let up soon, you'll never make it home today."

"I can try. At least get to town. I'll call you when I know something more definite."

"All right. In the meantime, I've had the men started on keeping cows fed and watered."

Tuck hung up. His boss needed him more than ever in a blizzard. Watering holes needed to be kept clear of ice. Hay needed to be laid out. Cattle pulled from ravines or drifts. A dozen other things to think about.

Nothing he could do from here.

Impatient with frustration, he turned and almost bumped into his hostess. Startled, he assessed what he saw.

She barely came to his chin, her shiny brown hair swirled around her shoulders. Her blue eyes were almost mesmerizing. He'd thought they were amazing when he'd first seen her in the swirling snow. Such a bright clear blue.

He stepped aside and looked away. He knew how beautiful women worked.

"I'll heat some water, we can have coffee or hot chocolate. What's your preference?"

"I'll take coffee," he said. "Do you have a phone book? I don't know Troy's number."

Troy Warren was a car mechanic in town who also offered towing services.

She opened a drawer and pulled out the thin directory and handed it to him.

Tuck dialed the number as soon as he found it. The phone was answered on the second ring.

"Is Troy there?" he asked.

"No, this is his wife Maisy. Can I help you?"

"My truck's slid into a ditch, I need him to pull it out."

"It'll be a long wait I'm afraid. There was a multiple car crash out near the interstate and he's there sorting things out with the sheriff's deputies. Might be there the rest of the day. You're safe?"

"Yeah. Anyone else there who could do it?"

"Nope, we only have the one tow truck. Where are you? I'll let him know when he gets in. But it might not even be today."

He turned to Jenny. "Where are we so Troy will know where to come?"

"I'm sixteen miles out of town, tell her Jenny Schofield's place. Maisy and I are friends. Troy knows where I live. Tell her he'll have to tramp in to let you know he's here, my driveway isn't cleared. Or let her know when he's done so she can call us and let us know."

He relayed the information and was promised she'd call back when Troy was on the way.

He rubbed his forehead again.

"He's out near the interstate. It might be a while."

"Then take the aspirin and have some coffee."

He swallowed the aspirin dry, then took the offered coffee and went to sit in the easy chair beside the fireplace relaying the rest of the information to Jenny.

It felt good to sit. He closed his eyes and leaned his throbbing head against the chair's high back willing the aspirin to take effect.

Jenny sat on the sofa and took a sip of her hot chocolate.

They sat in silence for several minutes. When he opened his eyes he saw she was gazing into the fire.

"Do you need to go into town? Maybe I could get a ride with you and then find someone to take me out to the ranch," he said.

"I wouldn't want to chance it. I just got back a little while ago and am glad not to have to go out again. I'm a private duty nurse and finished an assignment yesterday. Timing's perfect for the blizzard. No job lined up, so no need to worry about getting out any time soon," she said. "I went shopping this morning and had a heck of a time getting home. That was when the snow was only about five or six inches deep. Sorry but I wouldn't risk it now."

The phone rang. Jenny rose and crossed the room to answer it. It was the sheriff.

"Hi Tal."

The call was for routine checks for people living alone in outlying areas to make sure they were okay.

"I'm doing fine. I made it home from town before the roads got too deep. I have plenty of groceries, wood, and gas for the generator. And now I have a guest."

"Who?"

"Tucker Mason. He works at the Bar 7. His truck went into the ditch right across from my driveway."

"I've heard of him but haven't met him yet. Mackay thinks highly of him. I'll alert Albert when he plows to watch for the truck. Though who knows when he's going to make it out as far as you are. Are you all right with him there?"

"Of course. Why wouldn't I be? Plus I have Val."

"Right, no one would mess with your guard dog."

"Service dog," she corrected automatically.

Though most people looking at Val thought he was a K-9 with law enforcement training. Typical perception about German Shepherds.

"Call if you need anything. There's a pile up near Mumfrey's Junction, I've got a couple of deputies out there. Troy's on-site to sort out the vehicles. Two ambulances were dispatched. They're having trouble getting through."

"Tuck called Troy. Maisy told him it'd be a while."

"It's pretty bad at the highway. Troy's got his hands full. My guess is Tuck's going to be there for a long while—maybe even a day or two. This snow's getting worse and isn't stopping anytime soon. Stay safe and I'll check on you tomorrow."

"Thanks, Tal. You stay safe, too."

She hung up and turned to Tucker.

"According to the sheriff, you're probably going to be here for a while. The storm's getting worse."

2

Jenny updated Tucker on all the sheriff had told her.

He shook his head and rubbed the back of his neck.

"Sorry to impose on you."

"Not a problem, I bought a lot of food to hunker down through the storm, so there's plenty."

He nodded, took another sip of coffee and gazed into the fire.

Jenny finished her chocolate and went to clean up after her lunch. Might as well decide what to have for dinner. Since she had fresh produce, she wanted to use it first. She knew the meal she planned was tried and true for a guy—steak, potatoes and a crisp green salad. She hadn't initially planned on that for dinner, nor cooking for two, so she went to the chest freezer on the back porch and pulled out two steaks to start thawing.

When she came back inside, Tuck looked as if he'd fallen asleep. The cup was on the floor beside him, his head was leaning back on the high back chair, eyes closed.

She studied him for a long moment. He was more rugged than handsome. Definitely a man who, from the little she'd seen, had a strong sense of responsibility and duty. But he certainly wasn't chatty. Maybe he'd feel more like talking later.

When Jenny returned to the sofa she pulled her knitting basket near and picked up the sweater she was making for her friend Darcy's new baby. The teal and white yarns made a pretty design and teal was her friend's favorite color.

Val lay in front of the fire, dozing.

It was nice to be tucked up safely in the warm house while the weather raged outside. She continued to knit thinking about the new baby and how happy her friend and husband were with the pending arrival.

Tuck opened his eyes a little, watching his hostess knit. She seemed content in the stormy day while he felt antsy. The headache had grown worse. Maybe he'd done more damage than he thought. And the frustration of being isolated away from the ranch grew. He knew the work that would be needed to make sure the cattle came through the blizzard.

He should be back there working with the others to keep the herd safe.

The more he thought about what he could be doing, the more frustrated he became.

He felt a weight on his leg and looked down to see the dog's head resting on his thigh, his amber eyes gazing up at Tuck.

"Are you okay?" Jenny asked looking over at the two of them.

"Fine. I still have the headache."

He wasn't one to complain, but he wondered if she had anything stronger than aspirin.

"Not unexpected. You hit it hard enough to have a bump on your forehead."

He shrugged. "The truck wouldn't respond to steering, it swung around and then slammed to a stop with my head bouncing around like a basket ball. Not as bad as some falls I've had." Like when he was bucked off that bull and landed on his head.

Jenny brought him some acetaminophen and a glass of water.

"Try this. It's been long enough since you had the aspirin. We can alternate until the headache's gone. You're not showing signs of a concussion."

He downed the pills with the water and nodded. "Thanks."

The dog continued to stare at him.

"Is the dog okay?"

"Sure, he sensed something was wrong, that's all," she replied. "He's a trained service dog, to alert when someone is anxious."

She took the glass and nodded to one of the doors in the back.

"The second bedroom is sparsely furnished, but it has a bed. I'll make it up for you and you can lie down until your head feels better," she offered.

He nodded, idly patting the dog who remained by his side. Right now he had trouble thinking. The pounding in his head was growing worse.

"All set," Jenny said a few minutes later.

He opened his eyes and the room spun around. Closing them quicky, he groaned softly.

"Let me help."

A moment later her arm came under his.

"Just stand slowly, keep your eyes closed if you need to. It's only a few steps to the bed."

It seemed like a long few steps but in only seconds Tuck gratefully sank onto the mattress. She swiftly tugged off his boots and lifted his legs so he could lie down. Covering him with a duvet, she rested her hand on his forehead. It was cool and felt good against the pounding.

"See if you can nap. You'll feel better when you wake up if you can sleep for a bit."

Tuck nodded once, his eyes still closed. Lying down felt better. If he could stop his thoughts from spinning, maybe he could doze for a little while.

There was so much to do. He should be on the ranch pulling his weight. Not lying down in a warm cabin, isolated from everyone but one pretty woman and her dog. Maybe if he rested a bit he could go back to the truck to see if he could dig it out himself.

Tuck came awake some time later with the bump to the bed. Opening his eyes, he rolled his head slowly to the left and came nose to nose with Val.

"Is it time to wake up or are you just guarding me?" he asked.

The dog didn't move, his stare focused on Tuck.

"Okay, I'm taking it as time to get up."

He thought about it for a moment. Headache gone. Reaching up he touched the bump on his forehead. Still tender.

He entered the main living area a couple of minutes later.

"Feeling better?" Jenny asked.

She was in the open kitchen, making a salad.

"Yes, you were right, the headache's gone. Did Troy call?"

"No, no calls. I'll have dinner ready in about a half hour. Are you hungry?"

"Yes. Can I help?"

"I'm good here. You might replenish the fire," she said.

He took a log from the pile near the fireplace and added it. A moment later flames ignited the wood. The wood pile near the fireplace was low, evidence of the constant feeding through the afternoon.

He walked to the window to look out. It was already dark and he could only see as far as the light from the window spilled out on the porch. The railing was piled high with snow. He thought it was still snowing but it was hard to tell. So much for his plan to see if he could dig out his truck. It'd be truly buried by now.

"I'll get some wood," he said, noting the stack on the porch.

"I'd appreciate it," Jenny said.

He donned his jacket and stepped outside. It was windy, snow blowing on the porch, the stairs buried beneath the snow. He made several trips until the wood stand near the fireplace was fully stocked.

"It's cold out," he said when he came in the last time.

She nodded. " I've let Val out a couple of times. Glad I'm inside."

"It's later than I thought. Mind if I use your phone again?"

"Go right ahead, any time."

He called his boss to update him and was assured they'd manage without him.

When the call ended, he went to the chair by the fire and sat down, impatient with inactivity. If he was home, even with the bad weather, there was always something to do around the ranch.

"Want to give me a hand?" Jenny asked.

He rose and joined her in the kitchen. "What can I do?"

"Watch the steak in the broiler. I have potatoes in the microwave. Salad's made. I need to feed Val."

He leaned over to see two steaks sizzling beneath the broiler. In the summer time the men often had barbecues on the large grill at the bunkhouse. Jeremy did the cooking. Tuck wasn't a cook. Yet how hard could it be to keep an eye on the meat so it didn't burn?

They sat down for dinner as soon as the steaks were done. Tuck began eating.

Jenny watched him for a moment, satisfied the meal was to his liking. He certainly wasn't the chatty type she thought again.

"Things okay at the Bar 7?" she asked after the first pangs of hunger had been satisfied.

He nodded. "I should be there, but the men Mackay hired are all good workers. And Bill knows what to do." He looked up. "What do you do here to pass the time? I don't see a television."

"I'd need cable to see anything and it'd be expensive to get cable service this far out for just me. I used to watch TV, but being deployed, I got out of the habit and don't miss it now."

"Where were you deployed?"

He'd seen her in town a couple of times with her dog. And heard some of her story—she'd been in the Army which seemed totally bizarre to him. She was pretty, slim and seemed too delicate to be in the armed forces.

"I don't usually talk about it," she said, studying the food on her plate.

That he understood. He didn't talk much about his past either.

"You were a nurse there?"

Why was he pushing the issue?

"I was. When I got out, I came home. Now I take private duty assignments here in Wildcat Creek or in neighboring towns if needed."

"Because there's no hospital here in town?"

"Because I don't want to work in a hospital. If I did, the one in Coleville would be close enough to commute to."

He looked at her for a moment, but her gaze remained focused on her plate.

Tuck considered what she'd said.

"However did you get into the Army?" he asked.

She had soft shiny brown hair brushing her shoulders. Her eyes were that beautiful blue, her complexion ivory with a hint of pink in her cheeks. She wasn't that tall, was definitely slender, and didn't look anything like what he thought soldiers should look like.

"Enlisted like everyone else," she said looking up at him with a smile.

"You don't look like my idea of a soldier," he voiced.

"You'd be surprised how different soldiers can look."

"Was it your plan to make it your career?"

She nodded. "But one tour in Afghanistan ended that dream. I didn't stay in when my time was up—obviously."

Val came over and laid his head in Jenny's lap. She rubbed behind his ears and smiled at her dog.

"So you returned home when your enlistment was up? Doesn't the town seem a bit tame after what you saw as a soldier?"

"That's the main appeal. I grew up here. This is home. My friends are here."

"And family?"

She shook her head.

"No, my dad died when I was young. Mom remarried a few years back and she and her new husband live in Arizona. We talk on the phone and they visited a couple months ago. I've only been back six months."

"I'd think you'd head for Arizona when you heard of the storm. It's got to be warmer there."

Jenny shook her head. "Not for me. I had my fill of hot deserts. Are you finished? I have chocolate pudding for dessert."

Tuck was sure she'd deliberately changed the subject, but let it slide.

"I haven't had pudding since I was a kid."

Jenny cleared their empty plates and brought the pudding.

"So you don't get pudding at the Bar 7. I'll have to speak to Bill," she said in a teasing tone.

He gave a lopsided smile, imagining her standing up to his boss. It just might work.

"Tell me more about yourself," she invited.

"Not much to tell. I work on a ranch and sometimes slide my truck into a ditch."

"Do that often?"

"No, first time." He met her gaze. "And let's hope it's the last."

"Were you a ranch hand in Texas? Or just a rodeo cowboy?"

"A bit of both." He didn't want to go into that. "How did you get your dog? You call him a service dog."

She nodded. "He is. I have PTSD. He can sometimes alert to an attack coming on, but always be there for me if I get another episode." She looked at Val and he wagged his tail. "He goes with me everywhere."

"PTSD, what happened?"

"War," she snapped out. "I have more pudding if you want it."

It was as if she'd suddenly put up a wall six feet high. He recognized it and nodded. Time to stop pushing.

Once dessert was consumed, Jenny began washing the dishes.

Tuck added another log to the fire. The room was comfortably warm. He wondered if it would hold the heat when no one was awake to feed the fire. If he woke in the night, he'd add a log or two.

He turned back toward the sofa when the lights went out. Not an uncommon occurrence with a strong storm. Mackay's ranch had generators. Did Jenny?

"I'll have lights in a minute," Jenny said in the darkness.

In seconds the bright flame of a oil lamp flared. She put on the globe to diffuse it a bit and the soft light filled the room. In only minutes she lit three more, setting them in different places of the living area.

"I have a generator I'll fire up–to keep the refrigerated food cold. But it's not for the entire cabin. Which is okay, the lamps work. I just wish they didn't stink up the place."

"Tell me where the generator is, I'll go."

She looked at him for a moment, then shrugged. "I'll show you."

"You don't have to go out in this," he said.

"Neither do you. This is my place. I can manage," she said.

She'd pulled her weight in the Army. She could do so here, despite what that cowboy thought.

If Tuck had to describe her with one trait he thought it would be independence. He didn't know her at all, but she took a blizzard in stride. Invited a total stranger into her home. Power failures didn't faze her. Even got her back up a bit when he offered help.

Tuck took a deep breath, trying to quell the urge to do something. When was the last time he sat and didn't feel compelled to work? He wasn't sure he could do it. Maybe for one night.

"Okay, come on and I'll show you the generator," she said a couple of minutes later, going to get her heavy jacket.

Tuck donned his jacket and followed her out the back

door and around to a small shed attached to the back of the cabin.

She pulled the door wide and latched it open. Around the walls hung gardening implements and a hose. In the center of the small shed sat a portable generator. Flipping the lever from the power company to the generator, she checked the oil and gas levels. Satisfied both were adequate, she pressed the starter. The motor roared to life.

"Easy peasy," she said, stepping back.

"It'll run all night if needed," she said as they trudged through the knee high snow.

Drifts were even higher as snow continued to fall. Both had a light dusting covering their shoulders and heads when they stepped back inside.

Jenny took off her coat and went back to the sofa to picked up the knitting she'd been doing earlier. She glanced at Tuck. He went to the window again staring out at the darkness.

The silence was comfortable. Jenny watched as the small sweater grew. She pictured the baby that would wear it. Would it be a girl or a boy? Darcy had two of each, she didn't care, but Jenny expected Tom wanted another girl. He doted on those two they already had.

"Do you know when the storm's due to pass?" he asked.

She shrugged. "Last I heard we'd get a couple of days of snow so I don't expect it to ease up until maybe tomorrow afternoon."

"They'll be working on clearing the roads. Since Troy couldn't make it today, I'm hoping he'll be out first thing in the morning."

She ignored the tiny disappointment that sprang up at the thought of his leaving. She hardly knew the man. They'd just met. Would their paths cross again?

Now that she knew he lived in the area, maybe they could–could what?

Until or unless she could get over the PTSD, she knew it best to be on her own. And Tuck seemed closed off, not like he had a lot of friends. Yet, what did she know?

He could be married with a house full of kids for all she knew.

There was a big thump as a pile of snow dumped from a tree. Jenny jumped, startled. It sounded like the distant muffled sound of a mortar.

Thankfully no flashback. Val was right beside her and leaned against her leg, lifting his head toward hers.

"I'm good, Val," she said. She took a deep breath.

Tuck looked at them.

"He's attentive," he murmured.

She nodded.

"Sometimes sounds set me off. He's here to help me focus on the here and now. Snow dumping from trees can sound like distant mortar fire. And the fear it's coming closer will flood me."

She hated admitting the weakness, but talking about it instead of bottling it up was the recommendation from the doctor at the VA.

"Did you have snow in the part of Texas where you lived?" she asked, covering up her moment of weakness.

"Plenty in the winter. Which made the Blue Bonnets all the more plentiful come spring."

She thought she heard a hint of longing in his voice.

"So why leave?"

He returned to his chair and looked at her for a moment as if making up his mind.

"I'm one of four brothers. Not the oldest. My oldest brother, Tyler, will get the ranch when our dad passes most likely. After I figured out rodeoing can get a man killed, I decided to see different parts of the country. Mackay was hiring when I hit town, so I signed up. Been there five years now."

"Thinking of moving on to see more of the country?" she asked, fascinated by his story.

She loved her hometown, loved all her friends and the feeling of belonging. Granted, joining the Army had satisfied her yearning for adventure. Now that was in the past. She no longer had a desire to leave Wildcat Creek.

"Haven't thought about moving on in a long time. I like it here."

She smiled. "So Wildcat Creek's now home."

"Seems like," he said, as if just realizing it for the first time.

"I think I'll let Val out one last time and call it a night. Do you need anything?" she asked rising and crossing to the door.

The big dog quickly followed and ran outside once the door opened.

"No. Thanks for taking me in."

She wondered how hard it was for him to say that. He seemed more like someone who didn't like taking any help from anyone.

"I'm glad Val heard the crash. You couldn't know my

place was so close. You could have frozen to death if you were still in your truck."

"Naw, I'd have started for town. Someone would have been by."

Maybe. Or the road would be impassable and he'd have frozen to death half way there.

She was glad Val found him.

She put on her jacket and stepped outside on the porch. A few minutes later Val returned. Jenny brushed the snow off his fur. His thick coat insulated him and kept the snow from melting, not so in the warmth of the cabin. She knew better than to let him in to melt all over the floor.

They entered and Val went to the bedroom as if he knew the routine.

"I'll say goodnight," she told Tuck. "There are fresh towels in the bathroom, and a new toothbrush by the sink. Please turn out the lamps when you're ready to go to bed. And take one in the bedroom with you. Just be careful, don't trip and drop it."

He nodded.

She got ready for bed and placed a lamp on the bedside table so she could read for a little while.

The book couldn't hold her interest, however. Instead she thought about the stranger in the other room.

He intrigued her. Was it because she didn't know him like she did most of the people in town? She sensed a restless energy in him. She suspected he was a man of action and the inactivity of today had to be wearing.

What was he like being the foreman of the Bar 7?

Working long hours she suspected. Limited friends and hobbies. No mention of a wife or kids, so was work his main focus?

She smiled to herself, she couldn't see him with any hobbies unless it was rodeoing as he'd mentioned.

He didn't talk about his family. Only that mention of four brothers and that the oldest would inherit the family ranch. She wondered what spurred him to travel.

And how in the world had he ended up in an out-of-the-way town like Wildcat Creek?

She wanted more answers, but would he open up or rebuff any attempts to finding out more about him?

Most of the people she knew were from families who'd lived in the area for generations. Her own father's grandfather had first settled in Wildcat Creek in the early part of the twentieth century. Family was important.

Was Tuck close to his? From the little she'd learned, it didn't sound like it. But with the internet, it was easy to stay in close contact without being physically near.

She turned off the lamp and settled in the darkness. The hum of the generator was soothing as she drifted off to sleep.

3

Val woke her early the next morning as he did every morning. She considered him her furry alarm clock. He even seemed to have a snooze feature–if she rolled over and didn't get up right away, he was back ten minutes later nuzzling her as if demanding she get up.

"Okay, I'm awake," she murmured to the dog. Just once she'd like to wake up on her own. How late could she sleep if she had the chance?

Dressed a short time later, she opened the bedroom door. Val needed to go out and she'd start coffee for herself and her guest.

To her surprise, Tuck sat at the table a mug in front of him. The aroma of freshly made coffee filled the room.

"Did you stay up all night?" she asked as she and the dog crossed to the front door. Opening it to let her companion out, she noted it was still snowing and the depth looked to have increased another foot.

"No, I've only been up a half hour or so. I'm waiting until a reasonable hour to call about my truck again."

"With all the snow, it could take a while to clear the road to enable a tow truck to even make it out here," she warned.

"I know." He ran a hand through his hair. "I need to do something, though. I can't just sit around all day."

"How's the head?"

"Fine. Headache's gone completely."

Jenny went to pour herself some coffee.

"I saw a shovel in the shed last night. So I cleared off the steps and around your jeep. What do you do about the driveway? Do you have a snow blower?" he asked.

"Thank you. I appreciate it. No snow blower. Walt Nelson clears it for me or sends one of his men," she said referring to the rancher who owned the cabin. "But they'll wait until it stops so they don't come more than once."

"Doesn't the isolation bother you?" he asked, watching her as she pulled some eggs from the refrigerator.

"Not at all. It's why I chose this place."

Hearing the bark at the door, Tuck rose and went to open it to let Val in.

"Wait," Jenny called.

But it was too late. The snow-covered dog shot inside and then shook all the snow off.

Tuck stepped back, but not in time to avoid a major shower of snow.

Jenny laughed.

"Sorry, I tried to stop you. I usually wipe off the snow on the porch. It melts in here."

Already puddles were forming where the snow landed.

"Sorry, I didn't realize."

"Not that big a deal."

Tuck insisted on wiping up the floor while Jenny continued preparing breakfast.

She had just scooped the eggs onto plates when the phone rang. Quickly she hurried over to answer it.

"Looking for Tuck Mason," the voice on the other end said.

"It's for you," she said, holding out the phone.

Returning to the kitchen, she finished loading the plates and took them to the table. Putting his where he sat before, she sat opposite and began to eat. She didn't know how long his phone call would take.

The one-sided conversation didn't reveal much. Mostly cryptic one or two word responses.

He hung up and came to the table.

"Problem?" she asked.

"No, just one of the men asking for some direction. They can come get me if the truck can't be pulled free today. I'll call Troy after I eat."

"I'll check in with the sheriff's office to see if we can get an update on the roads," she said.

He nodded, attacking the food like he hadn't eaten in a week.

She was glad she'd made him a double portion. Now she wondered if that'd be enough.

Jenny finished eating before Tucker. She put her dish in the sink awaiting his and went to make the call. One of her friends was at the dispatch desk.

"Hi Helen, just checking in. Do you know the status of the roads?"

"Hi Jenny. The highway's being kept as free from snow as they can manage. I wish it would stop. County roads are being cleared in order of usage. Your's should have had one pass at least. Albert worked well into the night and is already back at it."

"It's more than three feet here I'm guessing. I wish it'd stop, too."

"Sounds right. I'll let the sheriff know you're okay."

"I'm fine. Any word on the power outage?"

"Half the area's out. No word on expected restoration. Line workers are doing their best, but apparently lines are down all over. We're running on generator power here."

"Okay, thanks for the update. Stay safe."

Jenny updated Tuck.

"If we got a pass on the road recently, it might be cleared enough for Troy to come out. I can check for you," she ended.

He nodded as he finished the rest of his breakfast.

"Hi Maisie," she said when her friend answered.

"I hear you have an unexpected visitor."

"His truck landed in a ditch at the end of the driveway. Any chance Troy can come this way?"

"I think he's on his way. He started at first light with some of the calls that came ahead of Tuck's yesterday. He didn't get home last night until after ten."

"Okay. Once we're done with breakfast we'll hike up to the road. Maybe the truck's sitting there already out of the ditch."

"Check it out and let me know. Someone clearing your drive?"

"Walt will, he usually sends one of his hands over when

he can. I'm not expected anywhere, so no rush for me to get out. He'll wait for the snow to stop falling."

"Lucky you. Stay warm."

Jenny hung up.

"Troy might have already been here. Did you lock the door?"

"No and keys are still in the ignition."

He rose and carried his plate to the sink. "I'll hike up and check it out."

"I'll go with you."

"No need," he said.

"Exercise. Plus Val will love the walk."

Ten minutes later the two of them and the dog slogged through the deep snow, sinking up above their knees with each step. The falling snow wasn't as heavy as before but still limited visibility. Tree limbs were bent low with the accumulated snow.

When they reached the road, there was a berm of packed snow blocking the driveway, evidence of the plowing service. The road was already covered with several inches of snow. They saw the white truck on the opposite side of the road. Troy had been and gone.

"Do you suppose he checked it to make sure it runs?" she asked as they crossed the plowed road to the truck. Val ran along the edge beside the berm of packed snow stopping every few feet to sniff the snow.

"We'll find out," Tuck said. He got into the cab and started the engine.

Jenny stepped back, looking for Val. The dog was several

yards behind the truck, sniffing something like dogs do.

The truck moved forward a few feet.

Jenny smiled and went to the driver's window which Tuck rolled down.

"It works." He stated the obvious.

"So it does. Good, you'll be home in no time. Unless you wind up in another ditch."

"There is that. I'll make it. Thank you for everything."

"Anytime. I'm glad Val rescued you."

"Do you need anything from town?" he asked.

She was tempted to invent something she couldn't live without just to have him come back. But that would only hold him up.

"I have all I need, thanks."

He nodded, then glanced at the dog. Val had come up beside Jenny and sat, looking at Tucker.

"Thank you, Val, you did good," Tuck said.

The dog barked once.

"Bye," she said, turning to walk back to her driveway. She was already missing him and two days ago she hadn't even known he existed.

When she heard the truck pull away, she looked after it until she couldn't see it any more.

"Well, he's gone," she told Val.

The dog looked up at her and then scrambled over the berm, trotting toward home.

The snowfall was light, the air cold and still.

Taking a deep breath of the crisp air, Jenny smiled. It had been a nice diversion. She wondered if she'd run into him in town from time to time now that she knew who he was.

She'd definitely look for him on her next visit to town. Not that it was likely to happen any time soon. She had to wait for the driveway to be plowed. And the snow hadn't even stopped falling.

The cabin seemed lonely when she and Val entered a short time later. Jenny glanced around thoughtfully. It had been a break in routine to have someone stay with her. Her mom and her husband had been guests last fall, but that wasn't exactly the same.

She wished she'd learned more about Tucker Mason. He sure didn't talk much.

"Oh well, let's finish that baby's sweater and when the snow stops, we'll take it to Darcy. The baby isn't due for a few weeks. Wouldn't it be great if it were born on Valentine's Day?" She talked to Val as she stoked the fire and then sat on the sofa pulling the yarn basket closer and taking up the knitting needles.

For a long time silence reigned except for the click of her needles. Val lay in front of the fire. Jenny added row after row to the sweater. She'd left it for last. Booties, a cap and a blanket had already been completed. She wanted to give her friend a complete baby set. It would come in handy for a winter baby.

After an hour, Jenny looked at Val.

"I wonder if Tuck got back to the ranch safely. It wouldn't seem too odd if I called to make sure he made it, would it?"

Val lifted his head, his tail wagging, thumping on the floor.

"I thought you'd agree. You rescued him, so he's special to you, right?"

The dog's tail wagged faster.

She laughed. "Okay, I'll do it."

Putting the knitting aside Jenny went to the phone. She looked up the Bar 7 Ranch and dialed.

"MacKay," a gruff voice answered.

"Hi, this is Jenny Schofield. I, ah, was calling to make sure Tuck Mason got back safely."

"He did."

"Oh. Okay, then."

"Wait and I'll transfer the call to the bunk house. If he's there he can pick up."

"Thank you."

Her heart beat a little faster. Chances were good he'd be out on the ranch somewhere–

"Bar 7," Tuck's voice answered.

"Hi. It's Jenny. I wanted to make sure you got home safely. It's still snowing."

"Made it with only a couple of skids, but none into a ditch," he said.

"That's good."

Now what. That had been the reason for the call. He'd made it safely. What else could she say?

"The truck ran with no problems?" she asked.

"No problems. I think the thick snow cushioned it when I slid off the road. I didn't see any damage when I checked it out."

She waited a moment.

He could pick a topic of conversation if he wanted to continue the call.

"Well, I'm glad. I thought you might be out on the range already."

"Heading that way. I only got in a few minutes ago. The roads are still treacherous."

"I won't hold you up, then."

"Thanks for the call."

"Good bye," she said and after hearing his goodbye slowly hung up.

"He's fine," she said to Val. The dog had come to sit beside her while she spoke on the phone.

"In a day or two I bet he forgets all about us," she said.

She knew it would be quite a while before she forgot the cowboy—if she ever did.

"Let's go outside and play in the snow," she told the dog.

No sense pining over something she couldn't have. Or someone.

By the time Jenny prepared lunch, the snow finally stopped falling. She spent a good portion of the afternoon clearing the snow off her jeep. She widened the path Tuck had made and cleared the steps again. Before she finished she heard a truck on the drive. Before long she saw Walt's big dually pickup truck with the blade on front, pushing snow to the side of the driveway. Time and again he backed up and pushed a fresh pile off to the side.

She waved and went inside to prepare hot coffee. He knew when he got to the house, she'd have something to warm him up. Pulling some brownies from the freezer, she heated them in a pan on the gas burner and had them ready when she heard his steps on the porch.

Opening the door she smiled at her landlord.

"Thank you, Walt. I'd be here until summer if you didn't clear the driveway," she said with a quick hug for him.

"Hey, gotta make sure you're mobile if you get a call."

"Come in and have some hot coffee. I have brownies," she said.

He stomped off the snow on the porch and stepped in. Taking off his jacket, he joined her at the table. A steaming cup of hot coffee awaited beside the plate of brownies.

"You okay?" he asked, sitting down and taking a sip of the hot beverage. Then he helped himself to a brownie.

"Doing fine. Everything okay at your place?"

"Lot of snow. The men are out making sure the cattle are okay. Wish we'd have a warm spell, but January isn't known for warm weather. At least more snow isn't in the immediate forecast."

"That's good. Have you heard when power will be back on? I'm still running the generator."

"Haven't heard. When it is then we'll know."

She smiled and nodded. That was the way of things out this way.

"Heard you rescued one of Bill Mackay's cowboys."

"His truck slid into the ditch across the road. Val actually rescued him—he heard the truck I guess. Anyway, he's the one who led me to Tuck. Do you know him?"

"I do enough to say hey to, that's all. He's foreman at the Bar 7. Mackay thinks highly about him. I see him from time to time at the cattlemen's associate meetings."

She nodded. "I don't think I've seen him around town."

"Keeps pretty much to the ranch. A loner, I'm guessing."

"Sounds right. He certainly wasn't very chatty when he was here."

She wished she knew more about him. Probably never would. She should let that hope go.

"The brownies are great, thanks."

"Take the rest with you."

She rose and quickly came back with a plastic container.

"Do you want a to-go-mug of coffee? I have a couple."

"Naw, this hit the spot. I need to get back,"

"Thanks again for clearing the driveway. I don't need to go anywhere right now, but nice to know I can go if I need to."

"Take care. Call if you need anything."

"Will do. Stay safe."

She watched from the window as the older man backed around his truck, lifted the blade and headed back toward the road.

She's stocked up on groceries already. But she wondered if she could think of something else to take her to town. She wished she could come up with something that would bring Tuck there at the same time.

For a moment she fantasied about running into him, stopping to have coffee together, and learning more about the man who had caught her interest. Silly daydreams. She'd made it this far in life without Tuck Mason in it.

She wondered how she'd manage a relationship with anyone when she didn't know what would set her off into the dark realms of PTSD. Her mother had had a hard time when she was there and Jenny had an episode. How would a prospective mate take it?

Time would help, her therapist at the VA had told her over and over.

Would the episodes fade enough for her to take a chance on romance?

4

Two days later Jenny headed for town. She'd wrapped the baby present in colorful paper, and had it on the backseat. Val sat up in the front gazing out the windshield as he always did. The roads had been cleared once the snow had stopped falling. She was glad to be out and about after several days house bound.

After a short visit with Darcy, who loved the baby set, Jenny headed for the post office. She didn't get a lot of mail, but what came for her went to her post office box. Mail wasn't delivered out as far as she lived.

When she entered the lobby, she glanced to the left. Beyond the glass door to the counter area stood Tuck Mason. She'd thought about him endlessly over the last few days. She really didn't expect him to be in town when she was–yet there he was.

She watched for a moment, until someone entered the post office behind her.

"Sorry," she muttered, moving out of the way and turning to her box.

Pulling out the fliers and junk mail, she quickly dumped what she didn't need in the nearby bin. There was a letter from one of her Army buddies and a couple of bills. She turned to leave at the same moment Tuck came out of the counter area carrying a large box.

"Hi," Jenny said brightly.

Val barked in friendly greeting, his tail wagging.

"Jenny, Val," he said with a slight smile.

"Let me get the door," she said, pulling it wide so he could go through with the package.

"Thanks."

He walked out and turned right, heading for the familiar white truck. Jenny's jeep was to the left.

"Want a cup of coffee?" she asked not even thinking, except she hoped he'd want to spend a little time with her.

He turned slightly. "I'm headed back to the ranch. This is a part for one of our pumps which gave out. Wouldn't you know it, right when we need it most."

She smiled and nodded. Disappointed, she turned toward her jeep.

"I guess I could take time for a quick cup," Tuck called behind her.

Tuck had no business doing that, but the disappointment on her face when he said no was more than he could stand. It wouldn't hurt anything if he took a half hour or so before heading back to the ranch. He'd thought about her a lot the last couple of days. More than he should.

She spun around, a bright smile on her face.

He felt a catch in his chest and frowned, focusing on Val. The dog stayed right by her side. He was wearing a service vest this morning and looked to be on full alert.

"At the café?" he asked. Putting the box in the back of his truck, he turned and walked toward her.

She seemed to hesitate a moment, then nodded. "Okay."

"Val can go in, right?"

She nodded. "He can go anywhere I go."

Tuck didn't say anything as they walked the short distance to Rosie's Café. The day was slightly overcast, but he felt as if it had brightened considerably.

Rosie's Café was a town favorite. Right in the heart of town, it opened early and closed late. Ranchers, teenagers, and everyone in between frequented the café at various times during the day. Now at mid-morning, there were few folks and plenty of empty places to sit.

They sat at a booth on the side. Val immediately went in under the table, turned and lay down, his face on his paws right next to Jenny's feet. Tuck sat opposite Jenny.

"Hi Jenny. I haven't seen you in a while. What'll you have?" Carrie Sue smiled at Jenny and then Tuck as she stopped by the table. Carrie Sue was the granddaughter of the cafe's owner and chief cook. She'd been a waitress in the café ever since her grandmother became ill and later died.

"I'm doing good. It's nice to be out after that storm," Jenny replied. "Hot chocolate for me."

Carrie Sue nodded and looked at Tuck.

"I'll have coffee," he said.

"Be right back," Carrie Sue said, turning to walk behind the counter and get two cups and the coffee.

For a moment there was silence in the booth, then both started talking at once.

"Sorry," Jenny said when they both stopped. "You first."

"I was asking how you were. Obviously your driveway's clear. The cold's keeping the snow from melting."

"Walt cleared it the same day you left."

"Good. Did the power come back on?"

"Yesterday. How are things on the Bar 7?" she asked.

Maybe she could find out more about him if he talked about his work. Didn't guys like that?

"Fine."

Well, maybe not all guys.

Carrie Sue returned with their beverages. She smiled at them both and walked back to the counter.

"Has the snow caused any problems on the ranch?" Jenny asked.

A group of boisterous teenaged boys spilled into the café. Laughing and shoving each other, they took two tables and pushed them together.

A loud crash sounded in the kitchen area as if an entire tray of cups had fallen. The teenagers dragged more chairs across the floor, laughing and shouting over each other.

Jenny jumped.

Val put his face in her lap, pressing against her legs.

Stress rose. Her heart rate increased. Blood pounded in her ears. She could scarcely breathe. She needed to get to safety.

"I have to go," she said suddenly. "Sorry. I can't stay."

She scooted out of the booth with Val right at her side. She grabbed for the leash and the two walked quickly out the door.

"Stupid," she berated herself as she almost ran onto the sidewalk, looking left and then right. She had to get away. Heading toward her truck, she began slowing down as she put distance between herself and the café. Taking deep breaths, she kept telling herself she was safe, she was in Wildcat Creek, not Afghanistan. She was doing her best to stay in the moment, not flash back to combat.

In the fall when she'd first returned, she'd met some friends at the café and managed fine. But the weather had been nice and they'd sat on the outside patio.

And no explosive noise had interrupted from the kitchen, or the sound of chairs dragging.

"Jenny," Tuck caught up with her and put his hand on her arm, gently pulling her to a stop.

"You okay?" He peered into her face, his gaze intense.

She took a deep breath and tried for a smile.

"Sorry. I, uh, it suddenly was more than I could deal with. I should have known. Enclosed space and all. I'm sorry."

"You don't need to apologize. I asked the waitress to make our order to go. If you wait here, I'll go back and get our drinks."

Embarrassed beyond belief, she wanted to vanish. She wished she had that super power. No, if she had a super power it would be to vanquish PTSD.

"I'm holding you up," she said, not meeting his eyes.

"I have time to spend. I'll be right back with our drinks. Wait here."

She nodded, feeling Val's weight leaning against her leg. Her hand tangled in his thick fur, she continued deep slow breaths, trying to reduce her stress. Trying to return to normal.

"Come on, we'll have a tailgate party. Sit on the back of my truck," Tuck said a moment later handing her a cup.

"Novel idea in the dead of winter," she said, walking beside him, the warm to-go cup in her right hand.

When they reached the truck, he let down the tailgate. It was still higher than she could easily sit on. Before she could even voice her doubt, he put his coffee down and picked her up and set her on the cold metal.

Sitting beside her, he looked at Val.

"Should he come up with us?"

"I think he'll be okay there," she said.

Taking a sip of her chocolate, she gazed down the street. Feeling embarrassed she wondered what he thought of her. If she could explain, maybe it'd help.

"This is why I live outside of town. Little things can trigger an episode. This time I felt stress rising when those boys came in. I have a hard time with loud noises whether it's voices or something else. Especially when they're unexpected. Like that crash in the kitchen. The IED we encountered was, of course, totally unexpected, then the gun fire."

She trailed of, focusing on her dog. She was in Wyoming. There was no danger. She was safe.

"Tough."

She nodded, glad he didn't try to offer some platitude or dumb advice.

"So I think I asked you how things were at the Bar 7. Did the snow cause any major problems?"

She desperately wanted the subject changed.

"Some," he said with a shrug. "And there're always cattle who get themselves in a fix. We didn't lose any, though."

She looked him in the eye.

"Care to elaborate?" she asked with a hint of impatience in her tone.

He returned her look and for a moment they had an impasse. Then slowly he began to smile.

"I can elaborate," he said. "I got back from your place to a bunch of steers in a more than foot of snow with no way to get to the grass below, so we took out hay. Broke the ice in a couple of water troughs, pulled a few cantankerous ones out of some gullies that were clogged with snow. Then one of the pumps near the homestead broke. I ordered the part and came in this morning to collect it."

"Are the cattle okay?"

"Yes."

"And you can fix the pump?"

"Yes."

She took a deep breath, holding on to her patience by a thread.

His eyes sparkled with teasing.

"I've fixed a pump or two in my time. If that's what you want to know."

She shrugged. What she wanted to know was more about Tuck and his life, not his abilities to repair mechanical things.

"Did you finish the baby sweater?" he asked.

"I did and gave it to Darcy this morning. She's about three weeks away from her due date. I think it'd be cool if the baby's born on Valentine's Day. That's Val's birthday, you know."

Tuck shook his head. "How would I know your dog's birthday?"

She grinned. "It's why he's named Valentine. He was born on February fourteen."

"And someone named a big German Shepard Valentine?"

"It's a perfectly fine name. A guy's name, remember Saint Valentine?" she protested. "Besides, he was probably a cute little puppy. Who knew then how big he'd get."

"True, but doesn't seem macho enough for your dog."

"I call him Val most of the time."

"I thought it was short for Valor–for your valor in serving."

"I didn't name him. He was almost three years old when I got him. He had to grow up and then go through service dog training. These are smart dogs, but they aren't born knowing how to be a service dog."

"I've heard the training is extensive."

She nodded, finishing the last of her chocolate. Should she ask for another–to keep Tuck a little longer?

"Finished?" he asked.

"I am. Are you heading back now?"

He nodded. "There's always work to do on a ranch."

"Thanks for taking time for a visit."

"It was my pleasure."

She smiled and hopped down, waving as she and Val headed to their next stop, grateful for the time spent with Tuck. And that he didn't seemed freaked out by her reaction in the café. Note to self: No more indoor dining. Strictly patio dining in her future.

Jenny stopped by the yarn shop before heading home. She wanted to begin a new afghan and picked out the colors to work with—bright lavender and deep purple. She didn't have a recipient in mind, but she enjoyed knitting. It was something she could focus on for as long as her attention span lasted. The PTSD had a way of making her restless and knitting soothed her anxieties.

She sang along with the radio as she drove home. Val barked a few times as if joining in. Reaching the cabin, she noticed how windy it had become. The remaining snow on the trees was showering down courtesy of the wind.

"This'll make it even colder," she complained as she got out of the jeep and faced the onslaught. Gusting stronger, it caused the trees to sway and more snow to spiral off.

Val jumped from the car and ran around the yard. When a burst of snow fell on him, he shook his head, looking bewildered.

Jenny laughed. "Watch where you're going or you'll be covered in snow," she called.

She felt a bit uneasy as she watched the trees sway. With this wind, there were bound to be broken limbs snapping off. Thumping sounds when large clumps of snow fell at once.

There were no mortars here. She took a deep breath. She could handle this. She just needed to focus on something else and not worry about sounds she couldn't control.

She was safe.

This wasn't Afghanistan.

She was not in a jeep heading to help wounded in a hot desert half way around the world. She was safe in Wyoming. Safe in her house as soon as she got inside.

Taking all the bags at once, she hurried inside, calling Val to come in as well. Once settled, she went into the kitchen to put the kettle on. A nice cup of hot chocolate would help. And maybe she'd warm some more of those brownies.

Distractions from the fear of flashback was needed. The psychiatrist at the VA had suggested ways to focus on the here and now and distance herself as far from the trauma as she could.

There had been no hot chocolate or brownies in Afghanistan.

No chance to knit or relax by a fire.

No kitchen to work in.

Val stood right by her side, leaning against her slightly. His presence was another comfort. And she knew if she did fade into a flashback, he'd pull her through.

But she couldn't resist the anxiety that gradually built.

"I'm fine. There are no IEDs, no mortar fire. I'm fine. We're fine," she said to Val, gazing into his golden eyes. He wagged his tail.

"I know. And you help make me fine," she said rubbing his neck and behind his ears with both hands. "And I'm grateful."

The afternoon passed slowly. The wind howled through the trees. True to her expectations, from time to time she would hear the crack of a branch. She'd jump in startled surprise each time. Steeling herself over and over to remain in the present, her stress level continued to rise.

Late in the afternoon the phone rang. Glad for the distraction, she answered it quickly.

"Hey, Jenny. It's Tuck. You doing okay?"

"Sure," she said, hearing the strain in her voice.

"The wind's almost gale force over here. How's it there?"

"Same. Trees are bending and swaying. Branches are dropping."

"You sure you're okay? Your voice doesn't sound like normal."

"Well, it's been a bit of a challenge not to flashback, but Val's helping. I'm doing the best I can. So far so good."

"I'm coming over."

"No, no need. It'd be a bear to drive in this wind."

"Expect me as soon as you see me," he said and then hung up.

"Okay," Jenny said to the dead phone.

She hung up and looked at Val.

"Tuck's coming over. What if I have a flashback while he's here? Maybe I shouldn't let him in. Maybe the wind will stop. I hate this!"

She paced the room. Picking up her empty cup, she carried it to the kitchen. Then paced back to the fireplace. To the window, watching the trees sway in the strong wind. Maybe if she could see them, stay in the present, she could avoid any problems if unexpected loud noises sounded.

Time seemed to stand still.

It was growing darker when she saw the familiar white pickup truck pull to a stop beside her jeep. The tall cowboy got out, carrying a box. The wind lifted his cowboy had and he slapped a hand on it before it could get away, holding the box in his other hand.

A moment later he was at the door. Jenny opened it though the wind almost snatched it from her hand.

"Come in," she said.

Val stood by her side, his tail wagging.

Pushing against the force of the wind, she got the door closed.

"I can't believe you came out in this weather," she said turning to smile at him.

She couldn't believe how happy seeing him made her.

"It wasn't as bad as it could have been."

He set the box on the table next to the sofa and shrugged out of his jacket. Hanging it and his hat on the hooks, he turned to look at her.

"You doing okay?" he asked.

She smiled brightly. "As good as can be expected."

Another limb snapped and she jumped. Val was right there, pressing against her, reassuring her.

"So I brought you some things. Four battery powered LED lanterns. They'll give you a lot of light when the power goes out and aren't a danger in causing a fire if you trip or drop one."

She smiled as she reached out for one of the lanterns when he lifted it from the box. Turning it on, she was surprised at how bright it was.

"Thank you, these will come in handy."

He pulled out three more and handed them to her. She set them on the counter in the kitchen, taking them out of the boxes. She'd put one in each room later to be prepared if the power failed with the wind. His timing was great.

"And I brought you a CD player and some CD's."

She turned, puzzled.

"Oh." That was unexpected. "Thank you."

Her voice must have sounded perplexed because Tuck gave that lopsided smile she liked so much.

"I could have asked if you had a play list on an iPod or smart phone, but I figured a woman who didn't have a TV probably didn't have anything more current."

"Hence the CDs."

He withdrew a small CD player with earphones. And a stack of CD's.

"I wasn't sure what you liked, so I brought my whole collection. I don't listen to them any more since I have moved into the modern world and have a smart phone."

She smiled at his teasing, still not understanding why he thought coming out in this weather to lend her his CD player was so important, but she couldn't deny she was delighted to see him. Nothing said earlier that day had her expecting to see him again any time soon.

"For the noise," he said, holding the player and earphones out to her. They weren't the small buds that fit inside ears. These looked like top of the line, noise canceling, full ear covering earphones.

She put them on. Instantly all sounds were muffled to a high degree. She couldn't hear anything. For the first time that afternoon, she felt herself relax slightly.

He handed her the stack of CDs and she looked through them, surprised at his choices. There were classical music CDs, country, which she would have expected, and some others she wasn't familiar with.

He reached out and took one from her hand, opened the player and inserted it. Pressing play, he watched as the music began.

It was an orchestra. She wasn't familiar with the song, but she could hear the different instruments and the cadence of drums. All noise from outside was gone. She was totally immersed in the rousing tempo.

The smile that lit up her face gave Tuck all the satisfaction he needed. He hadn't been sure how she'd take his coming over—or the gift. But seeing her now, he was glad he'd taken the chance.

Even Val seemed to relax his stance as Jenny seemed to grow more relaxed.

Tuck pointed to the sofa and she went to sit down. He sat on the chair by the fire and watched her. She closed her eyes after a moment, totally engrossed in the music. Val remained at her side, pressing against her leg. Her hand rested on the dog's neck.

A few minutes later her eyes flew open.

"Oh, Tuck, I'm sorry," she said, pulling off the earphones. "I've ignored you. Thank you for this. You don't know how much this means. I couldn't hear anything but the music."

"Actually, I guessed it might work. I have a buddy, a Marine. He has PTSD and when noise triggers are around, drowning them out with music helps him. I thought of you when I heard the wind."

"I never thought about doing something like this," she said, holding the earphones. "And I love this music, what is the song?"

He rose then stooped down beside her and opened the player. "Tchaikovsky's 1812 Overture."

"I didn't expect you to like classical music."

He looked up at her. "What did you expect, country only?"

She grinned. "Yep."

He felt a kick of something in his chest. Her smile was infectious. He'd like to see her smiling all the time.

"I like country," he said resuming his seat on the chair. "But I like other music, too."

"So I see from your collection. You can spare them for a while?"

He nodded.

"Is this wind making things worse on the Bar 7?"

"Not so much. The wind sweeps a lot of the snow off the flat part, so cattle can go back to grazing. Which means we don't have to find ways to get hay out where the cattle are at the crack of dawn every day."

"The wind's also blowing the snow off the trees."

Just then three things happened at once, the loud crack of a falling branch exploded, Val jumped into Jenny's lap, and the power went out, plunging the room into gloomy grey.

"Hold on, I'll get the lamps," he said,.

In moments the bright lanterns flooded the room with light. And the best part to Jenny's mind was no smell.

"That last one sounded close," he said.

She nodded.

All four lanterns turned on made the room almost as bright as the regular lights.

"And brought down the lines I guess."

The amount of light was wonderful. And the best part—no stink of burning oil.

"I guess. This is my first winter back and I didn't realize how fragile the electricity was this far from town. I don't remember outages when I was a kid."

"We don't get them very often on the ranch," he commented.

"Do you want to stay for dinner?" she ask. That last sound had been loud, but with other things going on, she'd been fine. Relieved not to have had a flashback, she wanted to extend his visit. She enjoyed the company.

"No, thanks, I better head back. Dawn comes early."

"Thanks for the lights and the CD player. I know it's going to help a lot."

"Good."

He put on his coat and hat.

"Do you want me to start your generator for you before I go?" he asked.

"That'd be great. Thank you."

Another few minutes of his company.

He left by the back door. In a couple of minutes Jenny heard the hum of the generator.

She waited a moment, but when he didn't return, she crossed over to the window. She saw the lights in the truck go on when he climbed in. He started the engine, made a three point turn and headed back down her driveway.

Turning back to Val, she smiled. "What do you think? I think that was amazing—he came all this way to offer something to help me cope with loud noises. I wonder if I can sleep in the earphones?"

The dog barked and wagged his tail. He went to circle in front of the fireplace and then flopped down.

"I don't know why you aren't burning up you get so close to the fire," she said. "Isn't it hot?"

Heading for the kitchen Jenny put on the earphones and clipped the CD player to her jeans. She continued listening to the classical music CD Tuck had selected. She planned on grilled cheese sandwiches and tomato soup. Comfort food. She was slicing the cheese when Val rose and went to the door, his tail wagging.

"What—"

The door opened and Tuck stepped in.

Pulling off the earphones, she looked at him.

"Forget something?"

"No, but I know where that last crack came from. There's half a tree across your driveway. Looks like it broke off about twenty feet up. Too big for me to move alone. Do you have a chain saw?"

5

She shook her head. "No. Can I come and help? Maybe together we can move it out of the way."

"I doubt it. Like I said, it's half a tree."

"Walt'll have a chain saw. I'll call him," she said, hurrying to the phone.

No dial tone.

"Not only the electricity's gone, so's the phone line."

He pulled out his phone and looked at it. "No service."

"Not out this far. Let's see if the two of us can move it."

Getting a powerful flashlight from his truck a moment later, Tuck led the way to the fallen tree.

The broken tree was clear to see. Its branches reached out a dozen feet from the trunk, and Jenny estimated the trunk was about a foot or more in diameter. She looked up into the darkness. Tuck shone the flashlight and she saw where the tree had split. The wind whipped around them, other trees still swaying.

"We can try pulling on this limb together, see if we can swivel it around enough to get the truck through," he said.

Both grabbed hold of the same limb and pulled. Jenny dug in her heels and pulled for all she was worth. The tree didn't budge.

"I need a saw," he said a moment later, letting go. "Or a couple of draft horses. Do you have a chain or heavy rope? I could try moving it with my truck, only I don't have anything in the truck that'll work."

"No, I've never needed any of those things. Maybe I should invest in a chain saw and some rope. Not that I know how to cut up a tree."

"Get a saw and I'll show you," he said as they headed back to the cabin, the flashlight illuminating the way. Night had fallen. The wind had not diminished.

"Guess I'll take you up on your offer of dinner," Tuck said as they stepped up on the porch.

"I wasn't planing much—soup and sandwiches."

"Sounds good to me."

They ate dinner and Jenny brought out the last of the brownies from the freezer.

"I'll heat them in a pan. Not as easy as the microwave, but it works."

"Or we can put them near the fire and they'll thaw soon enough."

Tuck took the foil wrapped brownies and placed them close to the fire.

"More comforts than camping," he said glancing around the room.

"Do you go camping a lot?" she asked.

"Not any more. I get outside enough with my work. We camped a lot as kids—even if only out near the property line. The ranch has a year-round creek running through one section. That's where we'd ride with bedrolls and all."

"Just your brothers or your parents as well?"

"When I was young, my folks came. Once we were teenagers, they let us go on our own. I don't think my mom's a great fan of camping."

"What's your mom a great fan of?"

He settled back in the chair and stared into the fire.

"These days I'm not so sure. I haven't been home in a long time. She loved putting up fruit and vegetables at harvest time. She was so proud of the rows of sweet corn, tomatoes, snap beans and preserves lining the shelves in the cellar. You name it, she probably preserves it. We had peaches and apple sauce, too. I can still see all the rows of jars with homemade labels segregated on the shelves in the cellar."

She heard a note of nostalgia in his voice.

That was unexpected from her tough cowboy.

"Don't you get vacation time?" she asked gently.

He glanced at her. "Of course."

"You could go see her again."

He shook his head.

So what kept him from going home, she wondered.

"Then you should invite her up here."

He gave that half smile she liked so much.

"I live in a bunk house with five other cowboys. Hardly the place a man wants to bring his mother."

"There are places to stay in town. My friend Darcy has a lovely room she rents out and the hotel's small but very nice."

He held her gaze for a moment. "It's a thought," he said slowly.

She longed to asked why he didn't go home, but that

seemed highly personal and she felt awkward asking. Maybe if they became friends she'd venture the question.

"I didn't go camping as a kid, but I have lots of stories about roaming all around Wildcat Creek and the adventures my friends and I got into," she said with a bright smile. "It was the best place to grow up. We'd raft down the creek, from above Palmer's all the way past town and on to McKenzie's ranch. We'd get out there and someone would always give us a lift back to town."

"What kind of raft?"

"The best kind—the ones we made ourselves, of course," she said with a grin.

Jenny spent the next half hour reminiscing about the adventures she'd experienced growing up. Recalling different escapades with different friends while some of the same friends featured in every one.

Tuck's gaze never left her face. He could listen to her all night. He wished he'd known her when she'd been a kid. Sounded like she loved exploring, trying new things. Fearless. Was that the reason she enlisted in the Army? For more adventures?

He could picture her there, blazing into any situation needing her help, fearless. Until— Until something happened to cause her to leave the Army and have flashbacks that could paralyze.

She tilted her head looking at him. "Well?"

He blinked. He'd been caught up in his thoughts. Had he missed the last bit?

"Well, what?"

"What was the most daring thing you did as a kid? Have you been listening to me?"

He nodded. "But I don't think I ever went into the pasture where a rampant bull was. You're lucky you're still alive."

She laughed. "I know. That was one of the scariest things I've ever done. But when Tal double dog dared me, what else could I do?"

He knew the sheriff slightly. What would it be like to grow up around all your friends, to see what they'd become as adults? To share a common background and a future that seemed secure.

At one time he'd thought he'd live in his hometown all his life. He knew his brother Tyler would likely get the ranch—or at least be majority shareholder if his dad went that way. But he never expected to leave.

And not return for more than a decade.

"Tuck?"

He blinked and focused on Jenny.

"What?"

"I'd offer a penny for your thoughts but I'm thinking you're miles away and a penny isn't enough."

"I was thinking how things don't always work out the way we think they will when we're kids. You're lucky to still have friends you grew up with. Shared memories will be with you for as long as you all live."

"Well, that's philosophical. You have friends who you share memories with."

"Even if I returned home, there's a gap."

Not that he was going back.

"Me, too. Six years in the Army. Not one of my friends came with me."

He didn't want to pursue this topic.

"I'm going to try the phone again. Let my boss know where I am," he said.

A minute later he hung up. "Still dead."

"If he worries because you don't come back, what'll he do?"

"I don't think he'll realize I'm not there until morning. Then I guess he'll call my cell to see where I am."

"Maybe he'll start a search for you and send the sheriff out here to see if you're here."

"Why would he do that?"

She shrugged. "I don't know. Just a thought."

"Unlikely. Come daylight, I'll head for town. Someone's bound to come along to give me a lift."

"Walt's driveway is only a mile or so beyond mine. We could hike over there and get his help."

"Good idea. That beats the possibility of a sixteen mile hike to town."

"Okay, then, we have a plan. Do you want anything else to eat or drink?"

"Another cup of hot chocolate?"

While Jenny made them both another cup of hot chocolate, Tuck replenished the fire. The conversation over the warm beverage turned to more current events. Jenny asked questions about his work and he told her more about the Bar 7, the men he worked with, some of the funny situations cattle could bring.

It was late when Jenny glanced at the clock.

"I didn't realize it was so late. I'll let Val out for one last run and then I'm going to bed."

Tuck nodded and then went to try the phone again while she let the dog out.

"Still dead," he said a moment later.

"Do you need anything?" she asked.

"No, I'm good."

"Then I'm off to bed. The sooner we go to sleep, the sooner it'll be tomorrow. I made up the bed with fresh linens, so it's all yours," she said, letting Val in. The wind was still strong, the trees swaying and bending before it.

Talking with Tuck had focused her attention, the noises from the wind hadn't bothered her at all.

They both rose early the next morning. Jenny tried the phone again, but no luck. Tuck was ready to head out, but Jenny insisted they eat breakfast first.

"No telling when we'll get a chance to eat again, and it's a long walk to Walt's place. I need sustenance to walk that far in this cold weather."

A quick breakfast, dishes left soaking in the sink, and they headed out. Val ran ahead then doubled back as if to say what's keeping you two?

The wind was still strong. Branches were scattered everywhere. They walked through the thick trees to get around the fallen cedar, then stuck to the drive until they reached the road.

As they walked, they picked up fallen branches and tossed them to the side to make it easier to use the drive when they returned.

The road was clear, though snow berms still lined the sides. Turning in the direction of Walt's ranch, they walked in silence for a while. Val stayed on the side of the road, sniffing here and there, his tail high as he explored to his heart's content.

"He's well trained," Tuck said, observing the dog.

"He better be. He cost enough. Service dogs aren't cheap."

"I guess not."

They heard a car coming and Tuck reached out to pull Jenny closer to him and the side of the road. A big truck roared by, heading in the same direction they were.

"Too bad it wasn't someone who works for Walt," she said, feeling flustered as she stepped out of his arms.

"They could have given us a lift."

"Except for the wind, it's not that bad out. What else would you be doing this morning?"

"If I could get my jeep out, I'd head for town."

Another truck came by this one heading for town. The driver sounded his horn in friendly greeting.

They both waved.

"Maybe we should have flagged him down and gotten a ride to town," Tuck said, turning to watch the truck fade in the distance.

Jenny stepped right up to him.

"Walt's place isn't that far. Though I can see you'd rather ride a horse than take a morning walk."

"Oh, is that right?" he asked, looking down at her. She was close enough he could smell the sweet scent of her shampoo.

Her eyes sparkled up at him in teasing amusement.

Temptation proved too much to resist. He leaned over and kissed her.

A moment later Val pushed between them, leaning against Jenny.

It was hard to see who was more surprised.

They stared at each other for several seconds. Jenny broke eye contact looking at her dog.

"I'm fine, Val. Good dog."

She turned and began walking toward Walt's.

Tuck stepped up beside her. What could he say? Sorry? That'd be a lie.

Maybe he shouldn't have kissed her. That was a given. Yet for a moment he relished that sweet kiss.

Jenny cleared her throat. "The drive to the ranch is coming up," she said.

Val raced past them and started up the cleared drive, fences lining both sides.

"How far to the house?" Tuck asked. He couldn't see any building from here.

"I don't know. We have to get to that rise ahead, then you can see the house in the distance. I've never walked it, only driven. It doesn't take long in a car."

"Jenny—"

She glanced at him. "What?"

"Are we okay?"

"Why wouldn't we be?"

"Are you mad about the kiss?"

He still couldn't explain it, but it'd seemed the thing to do at the moment.

"Of course not," she replied, looking straight ahead. "Things happen."

Things? Things like kisses? He frowned.

He never was good at understanding women. Look at his relationship with Trish. Or what he thought was a relationship with her.

The wind felt stronger as they trudged along the drive. There were few trees on this side of the road to break up the force.

Tuck figured there was still a half mile to go when they reached the top of the incline. He could see men in the distance, some on horseback. It was a working ranch after all.

They were spotted before they reached the house and one man broke away from the others and rode out to meet them.

It was Walt Nelson.

"Jenny. What are you doing here? Where's your jeep?"

"Hi Walt. My driveway's blocked by a fallen tree. Power's out and so the phone. Do you know Tuck Mason?"

Walt nodded, touching his hat in acknowledgment.

"He stopped by yesterday afternoon and his truck's on the cabin side of the downed tree, too."

Walt looked at Tuck. "What'll it take to move the tree?"

"Couple of strong horses or maybe a chain and a truck. We couldn't move it ourselves and I didn't have a chain with me."

Walt let out a piercing whistle and one of the cowboys rode over to him.

"Need something, boss?" he asked.

"Get one of the other men and the two of you head for

Jenny's place. We have to move a tree from her driveway."

The cowboy nodded and rode back to the others.

"I'll get a chainsaw and we'll take my truck back," Walt said.

Walt's truck reached her driveway just as the cowboys rode up. They had ropes on their saddles. Walt had put a large chainsaw in the back of his truck.

Once at the tree, the four men made short work of cutting away the branches and hauling them to the side. Then they cut the log into six foot sections, and the cowboys tied ropes to the sections and their horses pulled them out of the way.

In less than thirty minutes the driveway was clear.

Jenny thanked everyone. Walt and his men headed out while Tuck and Jenny walked down the driveway to her house.

She wouldn't refer to his kiss. Though she'd thought about it a dozen times since he'd kissed her.

While watching the men work, her main focus had been on Tuck. If he glanced her way, she'd look at one of the other men, but her gaze would return to him after a couple of seconds. She fantasied a couple of times of them returning to her cabin and taking a coffee break before he left. Maybe even leaning closer for another kiss.

"You take care, Jenny," he said when they reached his truck.

His comment dashed that daydream. She knew he had to get back to the Bar 7.

"You, too," she said with a wide smile.

It almost hurt her cheeks, but not for anything would she let him suspect her feelings.

6

Jenny tidied the cabin and as a treat decided to go to town for lunch. She needed to get used to normal activities. Maybe if she did one normal thing a day, she'd get better faster.

She headed for the café. She'd get a bag lunch, then maybe a stroll around town, just to be out and about.

Carrie Sue smiled at her when she entered the café. It was crowded and Jenny was glad she didn't plan to stay inside. She took a deep breath and walked to the counter.

"What'll you have?" her friend asked, wiping the counter in front of Jenny and gesturing to her to take a seat on the stool.

"I want something to go. How about a grilled ham and cheese, with fried onion rings on the side."

"You got it. Won't take long. Take a seat until it's ready."

She wrote the order on her pad and ripped off the sheet, handing it in through the serving window to the kitchen.

"Jenny?"

She turned and saw a tall woman dressed in business attire.

"Patrice? Hi, how are you?"

Jenny rose and gave her friend a hug. She hadn't seen her since her return to Wildcat Creek.

"I'm doing well. I heard you were back. I should have given you a call. How are you?" she asked and glanced at Val sitting next to the stool.

"Doing better than I was six months ago. Are you still working at the bank?" Jenny asked.

"Yep, I made Loan Officer not too long ago. First female one in the bank," she said with a grin. "I'm not sure Mr. Taylor was all for it, but he made it official a few weeks back."

"Good for you. Lots of responsibility, though."

Patrice nodded. "I'm up to it. If I'd known you were coming in for lunch, I'd have taken my break later. I'm finished and need to get back."

"I'll call you soon and we can arrange something," Jenny said with a smile.

It was good to see her friend. They'd gone to high school together and shared many hijinks growing up. Then they had gone to different colleges and rarely saw each other.

Patrice pulled a card from her purse and quickly wrote her phone number on the back.

"This is my cell. Call me when you expect to be in town again."

Jenny sat back on the stool when Patrice left, glancing around and smiling at several people she knew.

She was glad she'd returned to Wildcat Creek when the Army didn't work out for her.

"Here you go," Carrie Sue said a few moments later handing her a brown bag folded at the top.

Jenny paid for her lunch and headed outside. It was tempting to stay in the warmth of the café, but she didn't want to push her luck.

She and Val returned to her jeep to eat.

As she enjoyed the hot sandwich, she seriously considered buying a chain saw and some lengths of chain. She'd get Walt or one of his cowboys to show her how to hook a chain to her jeep and if another tree fell down, maybe she could handle it herself.

Then she frowned. She didn't know the first thing about a chain saw.

She definitely should take Tuck up on his offer to show her how to run one. And buy one. She smiled in anticipation of talking with the cowboy again.

After her lunch, and a quick stop at the Best Bakery In Town, she stopped by Darcy's to visit her friend. She brought red velvet cupcakes, a favorite for both of them and Darcy's children. The kids swarmed around her and she doled out the cupcakes once they all sat at the table.

"Such a treat," Darcy said once the kids had been cleaned up and sent to play in their rooms while she and Jenny went to sit in the family room. She savored the cupcake, thanking Jenny again for bringing them.

"What brings you to town today?" Darcy asked.

Jenny explained the recent events, –most of them, however she did not share about the kiss. It had been a spur of the moment thing. Tuck never indicated any special interest in her before or after.

Not that she wanted to become involved with anyone

right now. She needed to get this PTSD under control.

"Tell me more about Tucker," Darcy invited.

Jenny looked at her friend. "What do you want to know?"

"Do you like him?"

"Sure. He's nice."

Darcy laughed out loud. "Nice? From what little you've said, nice isn't the word I'd use to describe him."

"And what is the word?" Jenny asked.

"Rugged, exciting, interesting, intriguing."

Jenny blinked and stared at her friend.

"Where did you get all that?"

"Am I wrong?"

Thinking about it, Jenny shook her head. "But I never used those words."

"No, but you sound different when you talk about him. He's not from around here and that alone makes him intriguing. Look at all of us, we went to school together, we've known most people in town all our lives. Here comes a Texan. Why Wildcat Creek? Why settle down here? Why keep to himself? I've never heard of him and I've heard stories about a lot of the cowboys working the local ranches. A man of mystery."

Jenny grinned. "Hardly."

Yet her smile slowly faded when she thought about their conversations. He rarely spoke of his family. He hadn't answered some of her questions about his past, simply explaining his leaving Texas as he wanted to see more of the world.

He wasn't talkative as some men were. But she also knew

a lot of men who weren't talkative. She knew there was more in his past. Would he ever share?

"He kissed me," she said suddenly, wondering what her friend would make of that.

Darcy's eyes widened. "He did and you've been here almost an hour and are just telling me this now?"

"It wasn't a big deal. Spur of the moment, I think."

"And?"

"And what?" Jenny asked.

"How was it?"

"Unexpected."

Darcy gave an exaggerated sigh. "Next you'll say it was nice."

Jenny nodded. "It was very nice."

She grinned at her friend. "And over too soon."

"Did you kiss him back?"

"Not really. It was more a peck than a full blown kiss. Over before I had a chance to react."

"Ah, so now what—next step a full blown kiss?"

While Jenny wished for more, she wasn't sure she wanted to confess that to Darcy—even if she was a good friend.

"I saw Patrice when I stopped at Rosie's for lunch," she said to change the subject.

"If Darcy recognized the tactic, she didn't let on, but told Jenny about the rumors that had circulated when the last manager left and Patrice was promoted to the spot.

"She's done a great job, even if she was young when given the position. She is fiercely loyal to the bank, and holds her own when dealing with some of the ranchers around here.

"I told her I'd give her a call one day and maybe have lunch together. Want to join us when we do?"

"We'll see," Darcy said, patting her huge bump. "I'm hoping this kid comes early. I'd like to see my toes again."

Jenny drove home a short time later, feeling better for spending time with her friend. Halfway down her driveway she came face to face with Tuck's truck, heading out.

Both stopped.

Before she could even open her window, his truck began backing up.

Val barked, standing with his nose against the windshield, his tail wagging furiously.

"I know, it's Tuck. We'll see him in a minute. Be patient."

The dog began whining, pacing the small space on the seat.

Jenny's own enthusiasm at seeing Tuck also rose. How could she blame her dog?

Why was he here?

When she reached the cabin, Tuck pulled to a stop on the left side of the clearing, she pulled into her normal spot on the right.

She threw open the door to let Val sail over her to run up to Tuck. She almost envied the dog's blatant show of devotion.

Climbing out of the jeep, she greeted him.

"What brings you out here?" she asked going to meet him.

"I tried calling. Your phone's still down. I brought you a present," he said.

Reaching in the back of the truck, he pulled out a chain saw.

Jenny blinked. For a split second she thought he might have brought her cupcakes or candy or something romantic.

She smiled politely as he proudly held up the chain saw.

"I knew you could use one, so I thought I'd show you how to use it. There's that whole tree top that needs to be cut up firewood size, plus all the other branches that are lining your driveway.

Walt would have taken care of it all eventually, but she didn't tell him that.

"Oh. Okay. Let me take the mail into the house and you can show me how it works. Do you have time now?"

He nodded. "Plenty of time. I brought one from the ranch as well, so we can get started on that tree."

Snow still covered the ground. The wind had died down, but unless standing directly in sunlight, it was still cold.

"Wear boots or some sturdy shoes," Tuck called as she stepped up on the porch.

Ten minutes later Jenny was being instructed on safety features of using a chain saw. In addition to the saw, Tuck had brought a safety helmet, thick leather gloves and goggles. Taking his truck down the road to the fallen tree, he parked to one side. "We'll cut in rounds about sixteen inches long to take back to your place and then split it later."

She nodded with a smile. That sounded like so much fun. Not!

Still, she wanted to learn and he was here. Better cutting wood than being alone in the cabin.

Val ran around, venturing into the trees then turning to run back to them from time to time.

Once she mastered handling the chain saw, she began cutting off the smaller branches. Tuck pulled them away. Before long both of them were cutting the trunk in sixteen inch lengths to be split later for her fireplace.

It was growing dark by the time Jenny and Tuck finished cutting up the fallen trunk. He loaded the last of the rounds in the truck and they backed to the cabin.

Jenny's arms felt liked cooked spaghetti, trembling in fatigue.

"I'm not sure I can do another thing," she said, hoping she had strength enough to open the door.

"Go on inside, I'll stack these."

She nodded, wishing she had his strength and stamina. "Come in when you're finished," she said.

Once inside, she removed her jacket and all the chain saw paraphernalia. Heading for the kitchen, she washed her hands and put the kettle on. Something hot–preferable with lots of sugar–was needed.

Val came in with her and danced around. She fed him. She'd offer dinner to Tuck, but wasn't sure what she had. She'd planned on a light supper. But after all that work, she wanted something more substantial.

He knocked and then opened the door, seeming to fill the space. Jenny looked up and caught he breath. He looked amazing. Not as if they'd just spent hours cutting up a tree. And for him probably after hours of work on the ranch.

"Want to stay for supper?" she asked.

He nodded, "Sounds good."

"I don't know what'll it be yet," she said, turning to eye

supplies in the cupboard, then the refrigerator. Not enough time to thaw anything.

"Want to go into town?"

She considered it, then shook her head. "Thanks. If I can't find anything enticing, you can head out. But I think I just want to stay home now."

Her less than stellar experience at indoor dining reinforced her desire to keep away from stressful situations as much as possible.

Tuck went to build a fire while she tried desperately to come up with something that would satisfy them both. Spaghetti, garlic bread and a salad. That'd work.

As Jenny set the ground beef in the pan to brown and thaw, she began work on the rest of the makeshift meal.

"Your power's still out?"

"Yes and the phone. And no word when either will be back," she said. "Do you have power at the ranch?"

He nodded and came over to sit on one of the stools by the counter. "And if it goes out, we have several powerful generators to keep things working.

"I just have the one. I had to refuel it this morning. It just keeps chugging along."

"Were you in town earlier?" he asked.

"Yes, I went in to visit my friend Darcy."

She told him about her day and when prompted, he told her about his, mentioning others on the ranch. She asked about the men he worked with and his short answers revealed a lot about each man even without a long convoluted description.

"Do you have your own horse, or do all the horses belong to the ranch,?" she asked at one point when he'd been talking about a cantankerous one who objected to being shod.

"I own three so I can rotate them for the rough work. Several of the men have their own mounts, the rest Mackay owns and the men ride them."

Jenny was impressed. She knew a good cow pony had years of training and were worth a lot.

She glanced at Val. He had years of training and was worth a lot–his weight in gold or more to her.

They sat at the table to eat. The spaghetti was plentiful and the garlic bread unevenly warmed from being near the fireplace to heat. Still it tasted good and from the amount Tuck ate, Jenny knew he liked it.

They took mugs of hot chocolate after the meal, sitting in front of the fireplace. Tuck took his usual spot on the chair next to the fire, while Jenny sat on the sofa. She'd sort of hoped he'd sit next to her, but then chided herself. They were friends. Nothing more.

And she wanted it just that way. Didn't she?

The phone rang.

"Oh, good, it's working," she exclaimed and hurried to answer it.

"Jenny, Esther Martin here. We have another assignment for you if you can take it. I've been calling all day and this is the first time I've gotten through."

The local public health nurse often coordinated in home nursing for the county.

"Hi Esther. The line's been down. You're the first call to make it through. What assignment?"

Esther explained the agency had been contacted for home nursing care for an elderly women who had fallen and broken her leg. The doctor was trying to balance the medications she was on which caused her to become dizzy and fall so she needed skilled nursing care for a few days until they were sure the meds were working as they were designed to and not giving her disastrous side effects.

"She knows about Val?" Jenny asked.

"She was delighted. Apparently all the time her kids were growing up they'd had dogs. She says she misses them now."

"For how long?"

"I'm not sure, at least a week. If you can take it, they'll bring her home from the hospital tomorrow morning."

"Sure, give me the particulars."

Tuck watched Jenny talk, taking in the way she seemed to almost sparkle as she talked to whoever was on the other end. Esther. From the one-sided conversation he gathered it was a new nursing gig. He wondered where and for how long.

Not that it mattered. He wanted to see more of her, but only because she'd become a friend.

Friends hung out together, he thought. Like this evening. After working on a project together, they ate and were settling in for a peaceful evening. He liked that she didn't want to go out and party every night. That she wasn't demanding to be the center of attention like Trish.

Whoa, where had that come from? He hadn't thought about Trish in a long while. Now he'd thought about her twice in a week.

He couldn't begin to compare the two women. It would

be so unfair to Jenny. She was light years a better person than Trish.

He looked at his watch. Time to head for home. He had friends among the men who worked on the ranch. He didn't need any more.

Yet his gaze was drawn back to Jenny when she hung up. Her smiled touched him and he gave a half grin back.

"New job. For Mrs. Sadie Burrows, 83, fell and broke her leg in two places. I start tomorrow."

"For long?"

She shrugged. "As long as I'm needed, but probably a week. I'll learn more once I meet my patient tomorrow morning. She lives in town, so I'll be staying at her place. She needs someone there full time."

"Then I'll head out. You'll need to pack."

He fumbled a moment with a piece of paper he drew from his pocket, then held it out.

"This is my cell. If you want to talk, call me direct. No need to go through the house phone," he said gruffly.

"Thanks." She took the paper and glanced at the number.

"Call me and let me know how it's going," he suggested.

"Okay, I'll do that."

She smiled as they walked to the door.

"Thanks for helping with the wood. I don't know if I'll be able to move tomorrow, but it was great to get that spot in the driveway totally cleared. And look at all the wood I'll have next winter to warm this place."

He nodded, putting on his heavy jacket and clamping his cowboy hat on his head.

"Goodnight, Jenny," he said, opening the door.

She stepped closer, reached out to touch his arm. "Thanks for coming by and for the chainsaw and all," she said.

He stared into her pretty eyes for a long moment, ignoring the dog standing beside them, the cold air roiling into the cabin. Without thought, he leaned over to kiss her.

This time she responded and his whole body went on alert.

Pulling back, he nodded once and stepped outside.

"Good night, Tuck," she said softly before closing the door.

"Just where do you think you're going with this," he growled to himself as he stomped to his truck. Behind the wheel in no time, he headed down the dark driveway.

Hadn't he thought earlier they were friends? Was he trying to ruin that?

Yet, she hadn't resisted.

He could still feel the soft warmth of her lips against his even in the cold truck. What would it be like to give her a full embrace, mouth open, tongues dancing kiss?

Would he ever raise enough gumption to try?

At the moment, much as he might wish to do so, he was growing to enjoy their burgeoning friendship and didn't want to do anything to jeopardize that.

7

The next day Jenny and Val settled in with her new patient. Sadie Burrows was a delight. Smart and funny, she minimized any discomfort she felt in being transported home and as soon as she met Jenny, she wanted to know all about her, her dog, what had been going on in town while she was in the hospital.

Jenny brought her knitting and found a kindred soul with Sadie. For much of the first afternoon at home, Sadie had slept, but once awake, she called for her knitting. The two of them sat in her bedroom and talked while knitting.

Needed solely for her nursing skills, Jenny was pleased to find there was another helper doing all the meals and cleaning. Dolores had worked for Sadie for more than ten years. Some assignments required Jenny to pitch in and help with household chores. This time that wouldn't be needed.

She'd asked and received permission to use the phone when Sadie didn't need her. So the second evening, after the older woman settled in for the night, Jenny went to the living room. Pulling out the paper with Tuck's phone number, she called him.

"Mason," he responded.

"Hi, it's Jenny," she said.

"How're things going?" he asked.

"Is this a good time to talk?"

"Yep. Hold on a moment and I'll head for my room," he said.

She could hear a television in the background. He'd said he lived in the ranch's bunkhouse. Many ranches had a bunk house for single cowboys, with a shared common room and individual bedrooms.

Suddenly it went quiet on the other end. He must have reached his room and closed the door.

"You and Val doing okay?" Tuck asked.

"This is a super assignment. My patient is adorable. Elderly, but feisty and determined to break all records in getting better. Do you know her? She lives on Timberline Street a couple of blocks off Main Street. Sadie Burrows?"

"No, I don't know her."

"I didn't either before now, though I bet we've passed each other in town many times. She knits. We could have bought yarn at the same time."

"Is she really sick?"

"No. She broke her leg in two places a couple of weeks ago. She's been in hospital care but wanted to get home. The doctor's trying to stabilize her meds and I'm here to help with that. It's light duty. And she loves Val. Her kids had dogs when they were little. I guess it's too much to have a dog at her age, but I sure am glad I have Val. And for more than just he saves me when I have an episode."

"We always had dogs growing up. I miss that here. We've

got a couple of cattle dogs, but they're working dogs and stay in the barn when not working."

"What kind of dogs?" she asked.

The next few minutes were spent in discussing various breeds of dogs and then the conversation moved on to other childhood memories.

Jenny was laughing at something Tuck said when Val rose and looked toward the back of the house.

"Hold on, can you?" she asked.

She put down the phone and hurried to Sadie's room. The older woman was awake and struggling to get her water glass."

"Did you ring that bell and I didn't hear it?" Jenny asked, crossing the room to get the water and hand it to her.

"No, I thought I could get it myself. I was asleep, then woke up really thirsty."

She drank almost half the glass before handing it back to Jenny. "I'm fine. I bet I could have managed. How did you ever hear me?"

"Val looked this way. I think he has super hearing. He heard a truck crash on the road at the end of our driveway during the snow storm."

The older woman looked at Val who was watching her attentively.

"Good boy. Was anyone hurt in the crash?"

"No, Val rescued the cowboy who was driving. Which turned out to be a good thing or he might have frozen to death in the storm."

Sadie settled back on her pillows.

"I didn't mean to interrupt your free time. I'm fine. I'll just go back to sleep."

Jenny patted her hand. "I'm here for you. If you need me ring the bell."

Sadie smiled as she closed her eyes. "I'll remember next time."

Jenny suspected Sadie was asleep before she left the room.

"Tuck?" she asked when she picked up her phone a minute later.

"Everything okay?" he asked.

Jenny told him what happened and a few minutes later they said goodnight.

Jenny's bedroom was next to Sadie's. She checked the locks around the house and headed to bed. She brought the earphones and CD player, but didn't want to shut out all sounds in case Sadie needed her.

Thoughtfully she looked at Val. Could she count on him if Sadie needed something? He was trained to help her, but he seemed to do so much more. She hugged him before getting into bed.

She read for a little while, then switched off the light. Thinking of Tuck, she smiled again at some of the stories he told about growing up. He seemed to have had a great childhood. What was the real reason he left Texas and hadn't gone back?

By midmorning the next day Jenny had her patient bathed, fed, and up to practice walking with the walker. The doctor said as soon as she was ready he wanted her mobile. Sadie was a willing patient and asked to see if she could walk all the way to the living room.

With Jenny at her side, using the walker, she made it, but sank gratefully on the sofa when she reached it.

Jenny gently lifted her broken leg and rested it on the ottoman.

"I did it," Sadie crowed.

"You did. And I bet it wore you out," Jenny replied with a grin.

"I might just rest here for a while. Do you mind getting my knitting?"

In no time they sat working on their different projects.

Her phone rang. Jenny glanced at Sadie before she answered it. She didn't want to abuse any privileges. She was here for her patient, not for personal phone calls.

"Hello, Burrow's Residence," she responded.

"Jenny, it's Tuck. I'm heading into town in a bit, can I get anything for you."

"Oh, hi. I don't know. Let me check."

She covered the receiver with her hand.

"I have a friend coming to town and he's offered to pick up anything we need. Do you need anything? I don't."

Sadie's eyes sparkled. "Well maybe not *need* precisely. But I wouldn't mind some of those cupcakes the bakery makes. The orange spice ones. It's been a while since I've had any and it sounds like a treat for an invalid."

Jenny smiled. "I'm having trouble classifying you as an invalid."

She spoke to Tuck and told him what Sadie said. He promised to get some and bring them by the house. Jenny gave him the address and then said goodbye.

"So, your beau?" Sadie asked.

"No, just a friend."

Jenny didn't meet her eyes, looking at her knitting. She began another row.

"I'm not really looking for romance these days," she said.

"And why is that? If a good looking man looked my way, I'd sure be interested," Sadie said in a teasing tone.

Jenny laughed and looked at her patient. "I expect more than a few men look your way."

"Not many around now that are my age. But I had a wonderful husband. Few could compare with him. I've had a great love that I cherish. What are you doing not being interested in romance? I thought every red-blooded young woman was interested in romance."

"You know why I brought Val, right?"

"Yes, the doctor was clear on that. You could freak out at any moment. And the dog will save you."

Jenny nodded, smiling at the non-clinical assessment.

"What man wants to be burdened with a woman he couldn't count on. Especially in this county."

"Ahh, but the right man would deem it a privilege to look after you."

"I don't need looking after," Jenny said with another laugh. "I'm perfectly capable on my own."

"So am I, most of the time. Doesn't mean I wouldn't like someone to talk to at dinner."

"I have lots of friends in town."

"So do I. You and me sound too much alike. I'm eighty-three, you're what twenty-five?"

"Twenty-eight."

"Way too young to be set in old lady ways. Tell me about this Tuck."

Jenny looked at her knitting again. She didn't want to give anything away. He was a friend, that's all.

"He's the one Val rescued from the snowstorm. He's the foreman at Bar K, Bill Mackay's place."

"Have you seen him since that accident? He sounds friendly if he's calling you here. How did he get your number?"

"He gave me his and I called him last night—just to let him know we were settled in here and that I was all right."

"Ummm, sounds promising."

"Just friends. And I'm sure he has no romantic interest in me."

"And why's that? Can you tell if he's courting?"

Jenny turned the row and began another.

"I could tell and he's not. He's really reticent about his past. He's from Texas and he'll talk about being a kid growing up on his parents' ranch, but then there's this gap and it's Wildcat Creek stories. Plus if a guy is courting as you say, wouldn't he ask me out or bring me presents."

"And he hasn't?" Sadie persisted.

Jenny took a breath considering.

"Sort of. Maybe. We met for coffee one day and I almost, er, freaked out as you said. I ran out of the coffee shop. I'm still working up to being able to handle extreme noise or stressful situations. Another reason not to lead a guy on."

"And was he upset?" Sadie asked, her gaze locked on Jenny's.

"No. Actually he got our drinks to go and we sat on the back of his pickup truck."

"That sounds sweet," Sadie said.

"Tuck isn't sweet. He's a cowboy. Tough and capable. They're all polite. I think it's part of the code of the west or something."

"Well maybe he's working his nerve up to bring you a present," Sadie said.

Jenny bit her lip. "Actually, he has, I guess I should say."

"He has?"

"Nothing romantic–some battery powered LED lanterns to use when the power goes out. And a chainsaw. And sound deadening earphone and some CDs."

Sadie studied Jenny for a long moment.

"And did you need those?"

Jenny nodded looking at Sadie.

"But they're hardly romantic."

"Maybe not," Sadie said slowly. "Or maybe. Sounds like your cowboy isn't much in the ladies department, which is a good thing. No one wants a randy guy around who can't settle on one woman. He obviously cares for you or he wouldn't have brought things that you need. Plus after a polite thank you for rescuing him, he could have never been heard from again."

Jenny didn't respond, but thought about what Sadie said. She watched as another row of knitting covered the needle. Tuck wasn't her cowboy.

Did she want him to be?

Not unless the PTSD went away.

It might never completely fade.

Was she serious about spending all her years alone? No partner to do things with, no husband to build a family with?

"Do you mind making me a pot of tea?" Sadie asked. "Dolores will be back in time to make lunch, but I'd love to have a cup or two now."

Jenny was happy to comply. She had enough thinking about Tucker Mason for the present.

By the time the tea was hot and Jenny was bringing the tea pot and cups into the living room on a tray, the front door bell sounded. She quickly put the tray down in front of Sophie and turned to go to the front door.

"Maybe your cowboy," Sadie said, pouring herself a piping hot cup full of the fragrant tea.

It was Tuck. He held out a pink box from the bakery. In his other hand he held a bouquet of flowers.

"Cupcakes from Best Bakery in Town as requested and flowers for your patient," he said staring deep into Jenny's eyes.

Jenny felt mesmerized by the intensity of his gaze. Her heart kicked up a notch and she smiled as happiness invaded throughout her.

"Come in," Sadie called from the sofa.

Jenny held the door wide while he walked in and headed into the living room. She needed to get a grip. He was just a friend stopping by.

She followed Tuck into the living room and quickly made introductions. Sadie was profuse in her thanks for the cupcakes and insisted they all have one.

Jenny took the flowers to the kitchen to hunt for a vase. Then she brought another cup back to the living room. She set the flowers on a side table.

"They're lovely," Sadie said. "Thank you, young man, I'll enjoy them every day."

Tuck sat on one of the chairs near the sofa. His hat was on the floor beside him. He looked rugged and out of place in the feminine room.

"I'm glad you like them. I brought your orange spice cupcakes as requested and a few different flavors, as well."

Jenny opened the box. There were a dozen cupcakes nestled together, different colored frosting on each one. She tipped the box slightly so Sadie could see.

"Oh, they look so good. I'll take that one there," she pointed to one. "Then you each take one so I'm not eating alone."

As soon as Jenny and Tuck had been served, Sadie began peppering him with questions.

Jenny suspected what the older woman was doing, but kept quiet to watch Tuck's reactions. If Sadie could uncover another nugget of information, she was all for it.

Tuck was unfailingly polite. And seemed to take the questions in stride.

Then he turned the tables and began asking her questions.

Sadie laughed and responded with some wild answers.

Jenny was content to watch the two of them sparing with words. Neither one backed down. She was fascinated by this aspect of Tuck's personality. He certainly knew how to give as good as he got with her elderly patient.

After a half hour, Tuck checked his watch. "Much as I'm enjoying myself, I have work to do. I came here first, so I still have several places in town to stop before I head back to the ranch."

"Thank you, young man, for the cupcakes and flowers. I'll enjoy them both."

Jenny walked him to the door. Conscious of Sadie's acute hearing, she smiled and thanked him. Wanting to say more, but not be overheard, she smiled up at him.

"Call me tonight when you're free?" he asked softly.

"Okay. Even if it's a little late?"

"How late is late? Doesn't matter. Call if you can."

"I will. Thanks again."

He put on his cowboy hat and touched the brim. "Until later then."

She watched him for a moment as he walked to his truck, then closed the door, aware of the cold air she was letting in.

"Well missy, that young man is a keeper," Sadie said as soon as Jenny reentered the living room.

"He is nice, isn't he?"

"And he's smitten with you. I saw how often he looked at you, how he hung on every word you said."

Jenny laughed. "He did not. He's not the type to hang on anyone's word."

"Well, maybe not, but he's definitely interested. Now you need to get over your hang up about freaking out and let that boy know you're interested back."

8

Jenny thought about Sadie's advice as she was trying to fall asleep that night.

She wished she could just relax and see where life took her. She'd love to see where becoming more and more involved with Tuck might lead. There was so much she liked about him—and so much she wished she knew.

The basics were laid out in front of her. He was thoughtful, funny, strong, and compassionate. She liked how he was friendly yet respectful with Sadie.

Still, there was a lot she didn't know.

Would he ever trust her enough to share?

Could she trust him enough to share her fears for the future, her worries she'd have PTSD forever and that it'd cause her to harm someone at some point? So far she mainly cowered in a safe place and squeezed her eyes shut tightly. Val was there to bring her back. But what if—

Tossing and turning she tried to block her thoughts. She just wanted to go to sleep. Finally she did.

Sadie continued to improve day by day. Her medication balance had been achieved. No more dizzy spells. She made an effort every day to walk around the house with the walker as much as possible to build up her strength.

"You know that doctor wanted me to go to Holly Grove Convalescent Hospital," Sadie confided one morning as she and Jenny were walking around the living room. "But that's a place for old people. I wasn't going there. Not for me."

Jenny smiled. She could imagine Sadie setting the place on its ear if she'd had to convalesce there.

"I'm glad I was available," she said.

"Me, too. Okay, I need to sit a minute," Sadie said, slightly out of breath.

Jenny hovered nearby as Sadie went to the sofa and sank down.

"Whew, you're a slave driver," she said.

"Excuse me. Who insists she's almost all the way better and could walk to the post office and back?" Jenny asked, keeping an eye on her patient.

Sadie waved her hand as if pushing the question away.

There was a knock on the door. When Jenny opened it, she was surprised to see Tuck standing there, another familiar pink box in hand.

"This is a nice surprise," she said, opening the door wider.

"Hi Tucker," Sadie called. "Come in, boy. What's that box in your hand?"

"Cupcakes, Miss Sadie," he called back, giving Jenny a smile. "I hope it's okay to stop by."

"Of course, get on in here," the older woman called back.

"Fine with me," Jenny murmured, her heart beginning to beat faster.

She closed the door and followed him into the living

room. He'd already presented Sadie with the bakery box and she was opening it with a wide grin on her face.

He took off his hat and held it in front of him.

"Can you stay a bit?" Jenny asked.

"If I'm not interrupting," he said.

He shrugged out of his heavy jacket, putting it on the back of the chair and sat down.

"What brings you into town?" Jenny asked.

He looked at her and then Sadie.

"Uh, an errand. I had an errand and I thought I'd stop by and see how Miss Sadie's doing."

"You missed my walking, young man. Around the room like a speed demon. I'm doing great, aren't I Jenny?

"You certainly are. Pretty soon you won't need a nurse."

Sadie looked pensive for a moment.

"I don't want to go that far," she said. "I like having you here."

She smiled at Tuck and held out the box.

"Take one. Jenny can run get us some tea to have with the cupcakes."

Jenny jumped up.

"I can. Or would you rather have coffee?" she asked Tuck.

"Coffee if it isn't too much trouble."

"Ah, a man's drink," Sadie said, nodding her head.

Jenny almost laughed at Tuck's expression but continued to the kitchen to prepare their beverages.

She felt a bubble of happiness seeing him again. She'd wanted to call him the last two nights, but had hesitated. She didn't want to come on too strong. So far he'd agreed to being friends. She didn't want to risk that relationship. Take things slow and easy, she admonished herself.

Val pranced beside her as they went back to the others.

Sadie had obviously asked Tucker something about the ranch because he was talking about yield and beef prices and other things. Jenny sat quietly and listened, most of it going over her head. Many of her friends from school came from ranches and she'd heard talk like this all her life. Important to those ranchers, but not to her.

She was content to watch Tuck as he and Sadie talked. He seemed completely involved in the conversation. She liked the focus he brought. He didn't look like he wanted to be anywhere else but right here.

He glanced at her.

"Do you need anything? Either from town or from your place. I don't mind running out and getting something if you do."

For a minute, Jenny tried to think of something. That way he'd have to come back. But there was nothing.

"Thanks, I have everything I need."

"Well, I ought to be going," Tuck said. "Thanks for the coffee, Miss Sadie."

"Come and visit again young man. Jenny, you haven't been outside in days. Get your jacket and walk him out."

Jenny nodded, throwing a teasing glance at Tuck.

He put on his jacket, said goodbye to Sadie and waited by the door.

Val stood at attention by the door as if he understood

Sadie's suggestion. Once they were outside, he ran to the bushes and began sniffing.

"I really don't need to be escorted to the truck," Tuck said, setting his cowboy hat on his head.

"I'm happy to do so. She's right, I haven't been out except for a few minutes with Val, since I've been here," Jenny said. "It's still cold, I see, despite the sunshine."

"It gets well below freezing every night."

"I heard you and Sadie talking about the ranch, but not the day to day stuff. Things going all right with the cold weather?"

"As long as we keep check on the watering places to break any ice and let the cattle drink. Not much snow left which makes it easier for them to feed."

They reached his truck but Tuck made no effort to open the door. He looked as if he wanted to say something but was having a hard time finding the words.

"What?" she asked, intrigued.

He took a deep breath. "There's a dance on Valentine's Day at the Grange. Would you like to go? With me?"

She felt a warmth spread within her and couldn't help the smile that lit her face. Then reality returned. The smile faltered and she looked away.

"I would, but you know me. I don't think it would be a good match. Sadie has a word for it—freaking out. What if I did at the dance?"

"What if you didn't?" he asked.

She looked at him. "What do you mean?"

"I know you never know when you're going to have a

flashback and it's terrifying. But you have Val and you'd have me, and between us I bet we could keep you focused. At least we could do our best. And if a flashback happens, then it does. Please don't shut yourself away from everything in case of."

She bit her lower lip and looked at where Val was still sniffing around the yard.

"Unless you don't want to go with me. You can tell me straight out, I can take it," he added.

Her gaze flew to his.

"I'd love to go with you. There's no one else I'd like to go with, it's just–"

He brushed her hair off her cheek, tucking it behind her ear.

"Then just think about it. I'll pick you up at seven, we'd try the dance and if it isn't comfortable, we'll go right home."

Jenny longed to accept. She longed to go back to the kind of woman who could go out with friends and have a great time and not be fearful of flashbacks and nightmares and other lingering effects of war.

"Call me tonight," he said, leaning down a little to look her in the eyes. "I don't know when a good time is for you. I don't want to disturb Miss Sadie. So you call me."

"Okay. And thanks for asking me. I'll think about it."

Tuck leaned in a little more and brushed his lips across hers. "That's all I'm asking for now," he said.

He got in the truck and drove off.

Jenny stayed outside a little longer with Val. For now? Instantly she wondered what else he might have in mind.

She felt warm and bubbly inside from his brief kiss. Was it just between friends?

She had several male friends in town, from the sheriff, to some cowboys she'd known since school days. Not one of them had ever kissed her. And she couldn't remember ever wanting them to.

Not that Tuck had really kissed her. He hadn't wrapped his strong arms around her and pulled her in tight against his body to give her that kind of kiss.

Thinking of the dance, she wondered if she dare risk it.

By the time Jenny called Tuck that evening, she'd made up her mind. She'd take a chance. She wanted to go in the worst way and if he were game, so was she.

She blurted it out after he said hello.

"Great, I'm glad," he said.

She loved hearing his low voice on the phone—and in person.

"With the caveat if I need to leave, we leave."

"I said so, right?"

"Yes, you did. And Val comes."

"Of course he does. It's his birthday."

She laughed softly.

"Right, like he's always wanted to go to a crowded dance on his birthday."

"We'll stay on the edge of the dance floor so he's not in the way. People dancing aren't looking for a four legged critter in their way."

"Did you have dances like this in Texas?"

"Of course, ever hear of the Texas Two-Step?"

"Yes, everyone does it."

"And where did it originate?"

"Texas," she said, then laughed. "So did you have a special girl you took?"

There was silence on the other end. Jenny's good mood burst like a bubble. "Tuck?"

Had she said something wrong?

"Tucker?"

"Sorry. Yeah, there was a special girl. Once. A long time ago."

His voice sounded quieter than normal.

"Oh, sorry, I didn't mean to bring up bad memories."

She searched desperately for a different topic.

"Listen, I hear one of the men calling. Maybe we can talk another night."

Before she knew what happened, he'd hung up. Jenny held the phone a moment then slowly clicked it off.

Bad memories. A long time ago.

Maybe about the time he left Texas and never went back? What happened?

Jenny wondered if she dare call him back. Not tonight. But if he didn't call in the next day or two, she'd call him again.

She prepared for bed and took her book. But it couldn't hold her attention. She kept thinking about Tucker and wondered again and again what had happened. Her heart ached for the change she heard in his voice. She thought she heard regret or something more in his tone at the end.

The next morning after getting Sadie prepared for the day, Jenny checked in with the doctor. The medications had been working as directed. The dosage seemed to be working appropriately and Sadie was having no adverse reactions.

"So I won't be needed here much longer?" Jenny asked.

She enjoyed spending time with Sadie, but the last couple of days her nursing skills hadn't really been needed.

"Let's give it another day. If everything's the same tomorrow, I'll release special nursing care and you'll be free for another assignment."

"Okay."

Jenny conveyed the news to Sadie.

"Well, I expect you have more seriously ill folks who need your services. I'm right as rain now that the doctor has the right mix of drugs. Still need to have this leg heal, but time will take care of that. But I'll miss you, girl."

"I'll miss you, too, Sadie," Jenny said with a smile.

The two of them were in the living room, both knitting.

"I expect I won't make it to the Valentine's Day Dance," Sadie said sadly.

Jenny looked up at that. "You normally go?"

"Of course. It's one of the biggest events in town. Don't you go?"

"I did when I lived here before. But I only returned last summer. This will be the first one since I've been home."

"You going with that handsome cowboy?"

Jenny looked at her knitting, frowning slightly.

"Yes, he asked me. I said I'd go, but I'm just not sure."

"Go and have fun. That Tuck will take care of you," Sadie said.

"When I think about the dances in the past, they were

always fun, lots of friends there, like you said, it's a big event. But now when I think about it, I know it'll be crowded, people will bump into me, the noise will be overwhelming. I don't know. So far I haven't been able to have a meal inside at a restaurant. How would I cope with an entire evening of noise and stressors?"

"You'll have your dog and Tucker. If things get threatening, I bet that young man will whisk you away in a heartbeat."

"But what fun for him to have to be on the watch for a woman who could have a meltdown at any moment?"

"What if you don't?" Sadie asked.

"What?"

"What if you go, and are totally focused on having a good time, flirting with that cowboy, seeing your friends so that you don't have a meltdown? There's nothing in Wildcat Creek that's anywhere close to Afghanistan. What if you don't?"

"Then I'd have a great time."

"Right. Focus on that. Think of me, stuck at home."

Sadie gave a sad look and caused Jenny to burst out laughing.

"So we'll pick you up and bring you along. You couldn't dance, but you could enjoy the music, the refreshments and watch others dance," Jenny suggested.

"Be hard to resist dancing," Sadie said with a twinkle in her eye. "All right, I'll do it. But you better make sure that cowboy doesn't mind taking us both."

"I'll tell him he's the lucky cowboy who gets to escort two women to the dance. That is if he still wants to take me,"

Jenny said slowly. "In fact, I might have put my foot into it."

She explained to Sadie.

"Then call him. Invite him around here for dinner tonight. You'll be gone by tomorrow and I want to know more about him myself," Sadie said.

It was easy for Jenny to acquiesce since she wanted to see Tucker. She wanted to spend some time with him. She'd need to make sure he hadn't changed his mind about the dance.

It has been years since she attended the community dance at the Grange Hall. She and her friends had always gone once they reached high school–if they were home in February. Her last dance had been when she was eighteen. College and the Army had taken her away from home in February after that.

She expected most of her friends who still lived in Wildcat Creek would be there. She could picture Sadie sitting on the sidelines, making comments about everyone as she watched the dancing. Jenny already knew Sadie had a lot of friends from the phone calls that came each day. Two or three ladies had stopped by for short visits. The laughter from their conversations could be heard all over the house.

Jenny needed to keep pushing for normalcy. She had Val if things got dicey. She had Tucker who'd promised to whisk her away at the first sign of trouble.

And what if she didn't freak out as both Sadie and Tuck said? It would be nice to slip back into the social aspects of Wildcat Creek. She had friends she'd held at arms length since returning home. She'd like to spend more time with them. Maybe find some activities she could join in if she could get back to normal.

And if something did happen, she had her dog to help her through it.

She dialed Tuck.

The phone rang and rang, then went to voice mail.

"Hi," she said brightly, wondering why he hadn't picked up. "Sadie and I would like to invite you to dinner tonight. Short notice, I know, but I'm returning home tomorrow and she wanted you to come to dinner before I leave. Let me know if you can make it. I, um, hope you can."

Jenny hung up wishing he'd answered. Now she'd be on pins and needles all afternoon waiting to hear from him.

9

Tucker returned her call around one o'clock and accepted the invitation. Sadie alerted Dolores there'd be an extra for dinner then took her afternoon nap while Jenny took Val for a walk.

Jenny kept Val on a leash on the sidewalk. She'd enjoyed her stay with Sadie but would be happy to get home where Val could roam to his heart's content.

It was cold and breezy so they didn't stay out for long. The weather forecast called for dry weather for the next week. Glad for no snow on the horizon, Jenny knew her friend Darcy would be happy, too. If that baby came on Valentine's Day as predicted, she'd want a clear shot to the hospital.

Jenny set the table under Sadie's directions. The good china and silverware was used along with linen napkins. Jenny wondered what the rough and tumble cowboy would think of such an elegantly set table.

When he arrived, her heart fluttered as she went to the door. Opening it, she smiled. He looked wonderful. He'd obviously cleaned up for the evening. He wore new jeans, polished boots, and a dress shirt and bolo tie beneath his jacket. He held his cowboy hat in one hand, a bouquet of flowers in the other.

"For Sadie," she said brightly.

"No, these are for you."

"Thank you, they're lovely," she took the bouquet of colorful flowers. Where had he found them in early February?

"Come in. Sadie's in the living room. I'll put these in water."

Jenny put the vase of flowers in the center of the dining table and continued back to the living room where Tuck and Sadie were in conversation.

"I told Tuck he'd be escorting two of us to the dance," Sadie said with a happy smile. "He's glad to do it, too."

He nodded, looking at Jenny with a slight smile.

"I guess that gives me my answer," she said.

He frowned, not understanding.

"I was afraid you might have changed your mind."

"I plan to get better on this walker. I might be able to do some slow dancing," Sadie said.

"Don't plan on it," Jenny warned. "The last thing you need is to fall and re-injure your leg."

"My partner can hold me up," Sadie said waving her hand as if brushing away the mere idea of falling. "Tucker says all the cowboys from the Bar 7 are going. It's going to be a great dance."

"Unless we have another blizzard and no one can get to the Grange Hall," Jenny murmured.

"Hey, that's only happened once in the last thirty years. It won't happen this year," Sadie protested.

Dolores came to the doorway to let them know dinner was on the table. She sat next to Sadie while Jenny and Tucker sat together on the other side. The cook had outdone herself with the lasagna, crisp garden salad, garlic bread and red wine.

"This is mighty fine," Tuck told Dolores. "Better by far than anything our cook can produce."

The woman smiled in delight. "Thank you. Eat up, there's plenty."

"Tell us all about where in Texas you hail from and why you left," Sadie said once the first pangs of hunger had been satisfied.

"The ranch is in the hill country of west Texas. My great-grandfather branched off from a farm in Louisiana to raise cattle back in the early part of the twentieth century. Land was cheaper then, so the place is a good size."

"What kind of cattle?" Sadie asked.

"Polled Herefords with small herd of longhorns. Those are mostly for show," he answered easily.

"Mackay doesn't run longhorns, but he does Herefords, right?" Sadie asked.

Tuck nodded. "Winters are a bit harder here, but he does all right."

"Thanks to his cowboys, I bet," Sadie said with a grin.

Tuck nodded again.

"You ever think about heading back to Texas? To start a family maybe?" Sadie asked with a quick glance at Jenny.

"I reckon Wyoming's home now. I have no plans to return to Texas."

"Glad to hear that. What do your folks think about that?"

"I don't know."

Jenny felt the tension rise slightly.

"I'm glad you're staying here, too," she blurted out.

She wanted to change the subject before Tuck felt like he was getting the third degree. Sadie hadn't been so focused on her inquisition on his previous visits.

"And I appreciate your help clearing the tree from beside the driveway," she threw out, hoping Sadie would cease her cross examination.

"No problem. No more trees falling?" he asked.

"No. And most of the snow's gone, just some in shady areas left."

"Until the next storm."

She nodded.

"I have lemon meringue pie for dessert," Dolores said, rising and clearing her plate and Sadie's.

Jenny jumped up to help and carried her plate and Tuck's.

As soon as they finished eating, Dolores shoed them from the dining room saying she'd clean up.

Sadie headed for the living room, then paused.

"You know, I think I'm going to the back for a minute. You two go on, I'll be there directly."

"Can I help with something?" Jenny asked.

"No, no, I'll be fine. Go on."

Tucker led the way to the living room and waited for Jenny to sit down before sitting on the wide sofa.

"I'm glad you could come on such short notice," Jenny said. "Sadie wanted to see you again before I leave."

"Glad for the invitation. Dinner was really good. I'm glad we're going to the dance. I didn't expect we'd have a chaperone."

Jenny smiled. Val leaned against her leg watching Tuck and she rested her hand on his head. "You'll have a car full with the three of us and Val."

"Oh, about that. We may have to take your jeep. I only have the truck. And while you and me and Val might cozy up, I think that'd be impossible with Sadie and her cast."

"Okay, works for me. Shall I meet you here?"

"No, I'll come to your place and pick you two up and then we can stop here on the way to the Hall."

She nodded.

They fell silent for a moment, then Jenny said, "I'm sorry if I said something wrong the other night. I, uh, was just making conversation."

"Nothing wrong."

"Oh, okay, then."

He took a breath and looked at her. "Truth is, I haven't done a lot of dating over the last few years."

"Oh. Me, either, I guess. In the Army we'd pretty much go out in a group—especially in Afghanistan."

"You asked if I had a special girl. I did. Very special. Or at least I thought so."

Jenny wasn't sure she wanted to hear this. She'd been teasing when she asked the other evening. Now he looked so solemn.

He looked away as if it were easier to talk when he wasn't looking directly at her.

"We had just gotten engaged. We were going to a Fourth of July dance in my hometown to announce it there. A community affair like this one where almost everyone goes.

Only when I went to pick her up, she'd run off with my older brother."

Jenny stared at him.

"Run off? As in run off? Not just going to a dance with you, but actually left town together or something?"

He met her eyes briefly. "Seems they'd been seeing each other on the side, had a tiff and when I proposed, she said yes to get back at him."

"What about you?" Jenny asked, suddenly feeling sad for the man in front of her. How awful to find out someone wasn't who you thought they were.

"They left a note."

Jenny blinked. "A note. Like that made it okay?"

Tuck gave a half smile.

"I guess in their opinion it did. Anyway, it's partially my fault. I never saw it though my mother did. She told me she'd wanted to say something but wasn't completely sure, so kept quiet."

"So that's when and why you left Texas?" she guessed.

He nodded.

"I haven't been back since. I get Trish wanted Aaron, but to lead me on and have the whole town know it, pride I guess. I simply don't want to go back."

"And your parents, how do they feel about that?"

"I have no idea. I haven't been in contact with anyone since the night I left."

"What? What about your folks? They aren't to blame."

"No? My mom suspected and said nothing."

Jenny thought about it for a moment.

"That had to be hard for her. Isn't Aaron her son, too?"

He nodded. "So I figured that told me who she favored."

"Oh, Tuck, not necessarily. You need to give her a chance to explain."

"Do I? Why?"

"She's your mom for one thing. You only get one of those in life."

Val crossed to him and lay his head on his leg. Jenny rose and went to sit beside him, leaning against him slightly as if offering some kind of comfort, reaching out to take his hand and threading her fingers through his.

He looked at her.

"I don't need pity," he said harshly.

She looked at him and smiled.

"I know. But you're a friend. What can I do to help? Even Val senses you're upset."

"This is the first time I've talked about it. I've moved on over the years. It doesn't seem as bad now as it did then."

"Time heals everything or at least lets us move on. People change. As we grow up different things become important. Old hurts fade."

"True," he said, his other hand caressing the dog's ears.

"Would you want her back?" Jenny asked softly.

"Not in this lifetime. We were young. I've learned a lot in the years since I left."

He glanced at her.

"She was sort of clingy. I thought I'd like that, but now I'm not sure. If I were to get involved again, I'd want it to be with a strong woman, one to be a partner with, not someone to take care of all the time."

Someone like you, Tuck thought, keeping his gaze firmly on the dog. He hadn't thought about marriage since leaving Trish behind.

Yet wasn't that the normal way of things, find a mate, build a life together?

Not that he was thinking marriage. He and Jenny hadn't even gone on a date.

Yet they'd spent time together. Worked together. He felt he knew her better than he'd ever known Trish.

They sat in silence for a while and then heard Sadie coming down the hall.

The older woman smiled when she saw them sitting closely on the sofa hands entwined.

"I hope I'm interrupting something," she said with a wide grin.

"We're just talking," Jenny said with a smile.

"Ummm. So I have an update about the dance. I was talking with my friend MaryLou just now and she and Harry are going to take me."

"I thought you were going with us," Jenny said.

"I appreciate that, but I think it best to go with my friend and her husband. I'll see you there," Sadie said.

Sadie spoke about her long time friends for a while, then Tuck said it was time for him to leave.

Jenny and Val walked him to the door.

"You're going home tomorrow, right?" he asked as he put on his jacket.

"Yes. I should be there for a few days. I don't have another gig lined up."

"I could come out and start splitting some of that wood we cut up."

"That'd be great. I'll be there."

He nodded and opened the door, putting his hat on. He stepped outside then turned to look at her, cupping her face in his warm palms.

"I'm glad you're you, Jenny," he said softly then gave her a quick kiss.

"Goodnight."

She stayed at the open door as long as she could before cold made her close it.

"You okay?" Sadie asked from the hallway behind her.

"Yes. Sorry, I let all the heat out."

"You two have a chance to talk?"

Jenny nodded.

"Good. I'm going to go to bed. Tomorrow's a big day— I graduate to being on my own again."

"Except for Dolores," Jenny said.

"Yes, but she's been working for me for many years. We make a good team. I'll miss you, though, Jenny. It's been good to have someone around during the days and evenings."

"I'll pop around to see you from time to time. I'm not going anywhere."

"And, I was glad to hear, neither is Tucker Mason."

Jenny nodded with a smile.

As she prepared for bed sometime later, Jenny wondered if Tuck's heart had been shattered beyond repair.

Or had time healed it?

He'd kissed her several times. But never hinted it was

more than a spur of the moment gesture. And fairly casual kisses as kisses went.

She'd gone steady with Will Burson during high school, but they'd gone to separate colleges, separate careers. She still sent him Christmas cards, but what they'd shared so long ago had faded to a sweet memory of high school days.

She hadn't fallen in love with anyone while in the Army.

And upon returning home she hadn't dated.

No one sparked any interest until Tuck.

Was she falling for him?

Or had she already fallen? She climbed into bed and stared up at the ceiling. Her heart raced as she thought about every minute they'd spent together or on the phone. She recalled everything he said.

Could he ever think of her in a special way?

What would it be like to be Tucker Mason's special girl?

10

Tuck turned onto the familiar driveway the next morning. He'd cleared things with his boss to take the day off, so was ready and willing to help Jenny split the wood. It'd be until next fall at the earliest before it dried enough for her to use, but it'd dry out faster being split.

The snow was melting slowly since it had been above freezing for several days. Sunny spots displayed the undergrowth. There were still snowy patches in the shade.

He pulled in beside her jeep. The front door opened and Val ran out to greet him. Jenny followed a moment later.

"Good morning," she called, stopping on the top step. She wore a sweatshirt but no jacket.

"Want to come in for coffee before we begin?" she asked.

He got out of the truck and petted the dog. "How you doing, fella?"

Looking up at her he nodded. He didn't much care what they did today as long as he did it with her. She looked pretty as a picture even in jeans and a sweatshirt. He followed her into the cabin and shucked his jacket. The fire kept the room warm.

"No ranch work today?" she asked as she handed him a cup of piping hot coffee.

"Got it covered."

He took a sip and waited for her to sit down before taking a seat.

"Delegation?" she asked.

He nodded. "Routine chores today. I'd rather be here. Some of it gets old so I rotate and let one of the newer men handle things."

"And chopping wood doesn't get old?"

"It's a change at least."

As soon as they stepped outside, Tucker set up a large round to be used to hold the pieces he was splitting. He'd set a round on the bottom one then bring the axe down hard. Sometimes the wood split in half, other times the axe caught and he had to work it loose to bring it down again. Then he split the halves in half.

Jenny stood out of the way, but when the split pieces fell to the ground, she stepped in to pick them up and stacked them on the new wood pile she was building. They had a rhythm going and worked companionably for almost two hours before she stopped Tucker.

"I'm getting tired and you have to be ready for a break. I'll fix lunch."

He looked at the new pile of split logs and then at the remaining rounds. "Sounds good. We should be able to finish up this afternoon."

"I'm well on my way to having enough wood for next winter," she said.

Val had explored around then lay on the ground near the new wood pile. She called him to come when she headed for the house.

After washing up, Jenny began making roast beef sandwiches. She made two each and left the fixings out in case Tucker wanted a third. Getting chips from the cupboard, she placed everything on the table.

"What do you want to drink?" she asked. "I have cola, coffee or milk. Oh, and orange juice."

"Cola's fine," he said.

He waited for her to come to the table and held the chair for her, then took his seat.

"It looks good," he said before taking a bite of sandwich.

They ate in silence until all the food was consumed.

"Do you want another?" she asked as he finished his second sandwich.

"I'm good, thanks. That hit the spot."

"I have brownies for dessert," she said, rising to get the brownies.

She heated them in the microwave for a few minutes, then brought them to the table.

"Do you keep a freezer full of these?" he asked as he took two to put on his plate.

"Pretty much. I cook a batch when I make them and then freeze most of it. Otherwise I'd eat them all and be as big as a house. Plus Walt loves them, so I like to have them handy when he comes over."

"Walt's your landlord, right? Have you known him long?"

"He and my dad were friends. He's known me since I was a baby. I'm sure that's why he gave me such a great deal on rent."

"It's a nice cabin."

"If I remember right, he used to let one of his married cowboys live here. But they had another child and needed a bigger place. It'd been empty for a couple of months when I returned to town."

Tuck leaned back in his chair.

"Some of the other ranches have houses for their married cowboys. Mackay has a second house on the ranch. It's not used right now, but he said once it was for a married man if he hired one. Two of the men he has working for him now are married, but both live in town."

"Not as convenient as being right on the ranch."

"No, but more separation of work and free time. When you're right there, it's easy to be tapped to helping in some area if the need arises suddenly even at three in the morning."

The phone rang and Jenny rose to answer it.

"Hi, Mom. Can I call you back later, I have someone over."

She looked at Tuck and smiled.

"No, a friend. He came to help cut some fire wood. We just finished lunch."

"No, you haven't met him, but you can when you come visit next time. Can I call you back later?"

She listened a moment.

"I don't know, after he leaves. Maybe after dinner?"

She frowned and shook her head. "I don't know that either. But even if he stays for dinner, he'll leave after that and I can call you then."

"Okay, Mom, talk to you later."

She rolled her eyes at Tucker.

"Yes, I love you, too. Bye."

She hung up and turned back to the table.

"My mom,"she said unnecessarily.

"I gathered."

Maybe he should leave so she could call her mother back.

But Tuck didn't want to leave. He had the day off and wanted to spend it with Jenny. The whole day, not just the morning. From what he heard, she was okay with that. He might even wrangle a dinner invitation if he was lucky. Or would she like to go out for dinner?

"Thank you for splitting the wood," she said as she began clearing their plates.

"No problem. There's not much left."

She looked at him. "You up to it? You have to be tired."

When she looked like that, he knew he could go on for hours.

"Naw, it's a good workout."

She laughed softly.

"Yeah, like cowboys need a workout."

"Does your mother call often?"

"Once a week or so. She lived her most of her life in Wildcat Creek until she married Doug and they moved to Arizona. I keep her up to date on people she knows."

"And up to date on you, too," he said.

"That usually doesn't take very long. I lead a quiet life these days."

He nodded, then took a chance.

"Want to go out to dinner tonight and maybe catch a movie?" he asked. "We could go to Coleville."

She looked at him. "What movie?"

"I don't know, whatever's playing."

She smiled. "What if there's nothing we'd both like."

"Then we'll just have dinner."

"I'm not good in public places," Jenny said slowly, resting her hand on Val's head.

Tucker nodded.

"How about we try that barbecue place that opened on the outskirts of Coleville. They had a patio we could go to if things get too stressful inside."

"It's freezing cold and February," she said, laughing at the idea.

"So we bundle up just in case. Give it a try. Each time you succeed you're that much closer to being comfortable in public places," he said.

Jenny really wanted to go. She wanted her life back. She wanted to spend time with Tucker and do things couples did. This would be her first date since leaving the Army. Actually her first date in longer than that.

Dare she take a chance?

"Val and I will both be there for you," he said softly.

"Okay, but beware if I freak out like Sadie says, it's on you."

Tucker made quick work of splitting the remaining wood and as soon as it was stacked, both went inside to wash up.

It was mid afternoon when they headed for Coleville. The town was thirty miles from Wildcat Creek and about twice the size. Jenny was familiar with the town and had actually considered accepting a nursing job at the hospital at one time. Before the Army.

"It's a little early for dinner," Tucker said as they drove into the downtown area. "Let's see what's playing the theater and get the times."

The small theater in Coleville had four screens. Two had comedies playing, one had a kid's movie and the other was an action film.

"Want to see My Baby First?" he asked when they stopped by the marquis to look at the times. It was one of the comedies. He immediately eliminated the action film and kid's movie.

"Yes. It sounds like fun," Jenny said, checking the time. "If we eat soon, we can catch the earlier show. That way you won't be so late getting home after dropping me off."

"Not a worry, but that's a good plan. So now let's see if the hype around the barbecue place is justified."

They were ahead of the dinner crowd and Jenny was relieved to find the interior spacious with picnic type tables and benches and plenty of open space.

"You choose where we sit," Tucker said.

"Next to the window, then. It'll give me the illusion of freedom and beats sitting on the patio."

They went to a table and Val scooted underneath, resting his head on Jenny's feet when she took her seat.

Both ordered the ribs with baked beans and slaw.

Tucker watched Jenny glance around and then out of the window. She looked at him and smiled.

"So far so good," she said brightly.

"I hope the food's good. Mackay does a special barbecue sauce when he has his big event in the summer. I think you'll love it. We'll see if it's as good here."

Jenny nodded, picking up on the comment. Did he see them still doing things together in the summer? She hoped so.

"You're going to be late to call your mother," he said.

"I texted her before we left about the change of plans. I'll call in the morning," she said.

The waitress brought their beverages and some fried onion rings.

"The rings are included," she said putting the platter in the center of the table. "We have spicy sauce, Ranch, or chili sauce."

"We'll try them all," Tucker said with a glance at Jenny.

She nodded.

"These are great," she said a couple of minutes later as they nibbled on the crisp onion rings, dipping into different sauces.

The meal did not disappoint. The portions were so generous Jenny couldn't finish all hers.

She had a doggie bag, which Val kept sniffing as they headed back to the truck.

The evening turned out even better than Jenny had hoped for. She hadn't come close to having a melt down. The restaurant never got very crowded. The movie theater was almost deserted. They had no one sitting near them and the comedy kept her attention focused except when Tucker reached over to take her hand in his.

She could scarcely breathe for a moment. Her heart rate sped up and she glanced at him in the dark. He appeared to be enjoying the movie, so she tried to relax and enjoy it as well.

But for most of the evening she was acutely aware of his hand holding hers and her reactions.

When they'd left the theater, Tucker had reached for her hand again as if it was the most natural thing in the world. She smiled. She liked it.

"I should have left a light on," Jenny said when Tucker stopped the truck near the steps. The headlights illuminated the porch.

"We can see and once inside you can turn on a light," he said easily. He opened his door and Val lunged across him and outside.

"Whoa," Tucker said, surprised.

"Sorry about that, I should have warned you. He likes to be first out of the car. I usually get out really fast before him or he sails over me, too."

"Maybe he had to go really badly," Tuck said, getting out.

He walked her to the door. Jenny used the headlights to get her key in the slot and open the door. She stepped inside and turned on the light.

"Do you want to come in?" she asked, turning back to Tucker.

"No, thanks. It's getting late and I still have a ways to go. Tomorrow will start early."

"Thank you so much for today and this evening. I had a wonderful time," she said, stepping closer.

Would he kiss her?

"I did, too. We'll have to do it again."

She nodded. At least there was the likelihood she could begin to do normal activities like everyone else. She hoped so.

"Well, good night," she said when he made no move.

"Good night."

Val pushed against Jenny and she stumbled falling into Tucker's chest. His arms instinctively came around her, holding her close. His head lowered and he kissed her.

This time it was the kiss Jenny had been hoping for.

11

Jenny had butterflies in her stomach. She looked out the window again. Tucker was due to arrive any minute to take her to the Valentine's Day dance in town.

She'd had second and third thoughts, but was going through with it. Their dinner in Coleville had helped her to decide to stick with the plan of going. She'd made it through the meal with no stress or problem.

The movie theater had been a bit more challenging when it went dark, but she focused on Tucker more than anything and that had definitely brought her through.

Val sat beside her. He was wearing his service vest and knew he was working. He watched her as she looked out the window again and then walked back to the sofa. He kept by her side and sat when she sat. A minute later Jenny jumped up when she thought she heard the truck. Her heart rate increased.

Looking out the window, no truck. Val sat at her side.

"You know, this is going to be a different kind of night for you," she told the dog. "I'll be dancing and you'll need to stay on the sidelines so you don't trip anyone up. I'll be as close to you as I can be, but still—"

She hoped Val would stay when she gave the command. Normally when he was working, he was right beside her.

She looked at her blouse and the long dark skirt. This was cowboy country. Some women there would be wearing jeans and boots. It was February after all. She'd thought about it, but decided she wanted to dress up a little for Tucker. The long woolen skirt and lacy blouse would be sufficient if they didn't spend much time outside. Her jacket was thick and warm.

Val watched her.

"I know, you don't normally see me like this. I'm fine. A bit on edge but that's okay when going on a date," she said.

She knew her anticipation probably presented as anxiety to the dog.

"We're going to see Tucker."

Val barked as if in response to her comment. Did he understand? She thought he did.

The headlights from the truck washed across the window. He was here.

She took a deep breath and went to the door, determined to wait for him to knock so she didn't seem so impatient. She tried to envision every step he'd take until–

The knock came right when she expected. Taking another breath, she opened the door.

"Hi," she said with a bright smile.

He looked wonderful.

"Hi yourself," he said, letting his gaze roam down her taking in the long skirt and lacy blouse. "You look amazing."

Jenny smiled broadly, her heart taking another leap.

"Thank you. I just need to get my jacket and I'm ready."

Val stood beside her looking at Tucker, his tail slowly wagging.

"Hi Val," Tucker said. He looked at Jenny. "He's ready for tonight?"

"I hope so. We haven't been in any crowd since I got him so don't know how he's going to react. We'll need to stay on the sidelines and I'm hoping he'll sit and stay. As long as he can watch me, I'm hoping he'll be okay. Otherwise, we'll have to dance around him. This was not something that came up at my training."

"We'll manage fine."

The truck was warm and comfortable. Jenny tried to relax but felt keyed up.

"How are things at the ranch?" she asked.

"Same old. We've started preliminary planning for the branding in the spring, still some weeks away. And we've started a tally to know how many new calves there are."

"How do you know you don't count them twice?" she asked.

"We've segmented the herd. Count one group at a time. Several of us are counting, then we compare the tallies. Works pretty good. What did you do today?"

"I was called for another job. This one in Coleville starting on Monday. A new mother with a premie. She has health issues and so does the baby, so I'll be there for a couple of weeks or maybe longer. The husband couldn't take off work, so he'll be there evenings and I'll just be there in case they need me then. It's during the days I'll be working. But like most of my assignments, it's live in. Just in case something occurs in the night."

Tucker was silent for a moment. "Have you thought about getting a cell phone?"

"I don't have service where I live," she replied.

"But you would in Coleville or in even in Wildcat Creek."

"True." She looked at him. "Why would I need one?"

"To get calls when working?" he suggested.

She smiled. "So if my mom calls or something?"

He threw a teasing smile her way.

"Yeah, or something."

"I could get one in Coleville, I guess," she said slowly.

"Good," was all he said.

The parking lot was more than half full when they reached the Grange Hall. People were walking from trucks and cars toward the large building. As Jenny had thought, many women wore jeans. She saw enough wearing dresses or skirts to know she wouldn't stick out.

The large hall had been festooned with balloons and streamers in pink and white. The band was at the back, already playing. To one side were the buffet tables with the food for the evening. A bar beyond was doing a brisk business. To the left, a place to leave jackets.

Jenny was greeted by several friends she hadn't seen in a while. She quickly made introductions and in a couple of instances the men already knew Tucker. They all seemed interested in Val and Jenny had to ask them not to pet him as he was working. The dog stayed at her side, pressing slightly against her knee.

She spotted Sadie sitting in the chairs lining the wall opposite the buffet.

"I see Sadie, shall we go say hi?" she asked Tucker.

"Sure."

As they walked over, he leaned closer and asked softly, "How are you holding up so far?"

"So far I'm fine. It's fun to see people again that I haven't seen in a long time. I don't feel any stress just happiness."

She smiled at him and then turned as they approached the older woman.

"Hi, Sadie," she said when they reached her.

"Hi you two. And Val. Glad you came."

"Me, too. So far so good."

"You'll have a great evening. MaryLou and Harry are already dancing. You'll have to meet them when they get back."

As more and more people began to dance, Tucker asked Jenny if she wanted to.

"I do. And I have an idea." She removed Val's service vest and put it on the seat next to Sadie. "Can Val stay here with you?" she asked.

"Of course."

"Good dog. Val, stay." Jenny said.

Then she took Tucker's offered hand and followed him out to the dance floor.

The music was fast and lively. The dancing fun and invigorating. From time to time she glanced over at Val. He sat at Sadie's feet, his gaze following Jenny's every move. She smiled, pleased he was still watching her, but glad he'd stayed off the dance floor.

When a slow song began, Tucker drew her into his arms and began to sway to the slower rhythm. His chin rested against the side of her head and Jenny closed her eyes to enjoy the sensations sweeping through her.

She breathed in his scent, the hint of aftershave that smelled woodsy. She felt the strength of his muscles as he held her lightly against his body. She could stay like this forever. She hadn't known this man for long. Not like she'd known most of the people here tonight. But she knew her feelings for him were strong. Stronger than any she'd ever experienced.

She was in love. Whatever that meant for the future. Did he feel something for her? She thought so, but wasn't certain.

Sadie thought he was a special man who did thoughtful things instead of dressing up everything in flowers and candy. Could that be true?

There was no reason for him to give her the earphones and CD player to help reduce sounds that could trigger a flashback. That was truly thoughtful. He hadn't had to give her a chainsaw and show her how to use it. Some would think that an odd gift, but the more she thought about it, the more she liked the idea of his giving her practical things that would help her in the future.

Though she wouldn't mind a bouquet of flowers from time to time like the ones he brought her at Sadie's. She'd taken them home and enjoyed them for several days.

When the dance ended, he was slow to let her go.

She smiled up at him.

"That was nice," she said.

"It was. Let's hope they do a lot of slow ones. Do you want a drink?"

She nodded. It was warm in the hall after all the people filed in, not to mention the exertion of dancing.

He led her over to Sadie. There were several empty seats and Jenny sat in the one next to the older woman.

"Would you like something to drink Miss Sadie?" he asked.

She asked for a soda as did Jenny and he crossed the room to get the drinks.

"He looks mighty fine this evening," Sadie said, her eyes following him across the hall.

"He does clean up good," Jenny said, her gaze also on Tucker.

Sadie looked at Jenny. "You two make a cute couple on the dance floor."

Jenny nodded.

When he brought the drinks, they sat together and talked for a little while. Sadie's friends came to sit down and introductions were made.

The band began another song and Sadie smiled at Tucker.

"Texas two-step music. I can't see a Texas boy sitting this one out," she said.

"You're right. Time to get back on the floor," he said with a grin. He held out his hand for Jenny and they moved quickly to the dance area.

The evening flew by. Val grew more comfortable as the night progressed, even lying down at Sadie's feet, his gaze always following Jenny.

She never felt the slightest twinge of a flashback. She spoke with friends she'd known most of her life. Filling Tuck in with brief bios of the people he didn't already know. She spent some time with Sadie and relished every moment with Tucker.

Before she knew it, they were playing the final song. Tucker drew her close for the slow melody and again rested his head against hers.

"This has been a special night," he said softly.

"It has," she agreed swaying to the music. To think she'd been hesitant to attend. "Thank you for inviting me," she said.

"Thank you for coming."

She smiled snuggling closer. She hated for the evening to end.

But there was still the ride home. And maybe another goodnight kiss.

It was cold when they left the warmth of the hall. A slight breeze made it seem even colder. Jenny hopped into the truck when Tucker opened the door, Val jumping up to be with her.

"You did great tonight, fellow," she said, rubbing his neck. "I'm glad you were there."

And even more glad she hadn't needed his services.

The head lights from the truck shone in the darkness. Neither of them talked much on the ride out to Jenny's place. She was comfortably tired, having had a good night with visiting with friends and dancing.

"Are all Texas cowboys great dancers?" she asked.

"No one's ever said I was a great dancer," he replied.

"Then you've hung out with the wrong kind of gals."

"True," he muttered.

She frowned. She hadn't meant to bring up the past.

"But I'm hanging out with the right kind now," he said, reaching for her hand and linking his fingers with hers.

Jenny was content.

Tucker walked her to the door when they reached the cabin.

She invited him in, but he said he need to head for home, he had an early day planned ahead.

Unlocking the door she opened it to let Val inside, then turned back to Tucker. As if planned, he reached for her when she reached for him.

The kiss was all she remembered and more. She didn't want him to leave. She wanted him to stay forever.

"Goodnight," he said huskily a minute later, brushing her lips lightly with his thumb. "Give me your phone number when you get your new cell phone."

"I will," she promised. "Thanks again, I had a wonderful time."

"Me, too."

He tapped her chin lightly and turned to walk to the truck.

Jenny almost floated on air as she entered the cabin. It was cool inside, so she built up the fire and made herself some hot chocolate. She was still too wired from the evening to go to bed. Instead, she'd spend the time remembering every magical moment of the night.

She'd finished the cocoa and let Val out for one last run before heading to bed. It was well after midnight, but she was still floating and not at all sleepy.

The phone rang.

She went to answer it, always fearful when it rang so late at night.

"Jenny? Tal here," the sheriff said.

"What's wrong?" she asked, knowing something was up or Tal wouldn't be calling her.

"There's been an accident. Tucker's truck was smashed up good by some drunk. He's on his way to the hospital in Coleville with head injuries. Since the two of you were together tonight, I thought you should know."

"Oh no. Is he all right? Is he going to be? Never mind, I'm on my way there now," she said.

She grabbed her jacket, banked the fire, and snatched up Val's service vest. "Come on, boy, Tucker needs us."

Driving as fast as she dare, Jenny made it to the hospital in Coleville in record time. Every moment of the trip she'd prayed he'd be okay.

Val sat in the passenger seat, looking out the windshield. She tried to keep the images at bay. The last thing she needed now was another flashback. But she could imagine Tucker being banged up by a car crash. Not like an IED, she kept telling herself. He had a big truck, it could withstand a lot.

But head injuries? They could be bad. He'd hit his head when his truck had slid into the ditch. She hoped this wasn't anymore than that had proved to be.

It seemed to take forever to get to Coleville, but finally she pulled into the almost empty parking lot of the hospital.

She snapped Val's vest on him and let him out. Almost running, they headed for the ER.

Entering, she went right to the registration desk.

"Tucker Mason?" she asked.

"He's here. Are you family?"

"No, but a close friend. His family's in Texas."

Gosh, what if they needed to contact them? She had no idea where in Texas they even lived.

"The doctor's with him now, it'll be a few minutes. I'll let him know you're here."

"How is he?" she asked with trepidation.

"I'll have the doctor speak with you in a few minutes. Have a seat."

Jenny wanted to dash down the hallway and find the cubicle where Tucker was, but knew better than to push her luck. She hoped the doctor would talk with her as Tucker's friend but not family.

"Tell the doctor I'm a nurse. I can help Tucker if he needs it once he's discharged."

The receptionist nodded. "Will do."

The minutes stretched out, moving so slowly Jenny had to constantly recheck her watch to make sure time was passing.

Finally a young man in scrubs came into the waiting area.

"Tucker Mason's friend?" he asked approaching Jenny. She was the only one in the waiting room.

"Yes. Jenny Scholfield. How is he?" she asked rising.

Val stood when she did.

The doctor looked at the dog and then Jenny. "I've heard of you, you're the Army nurse with PTSD who still takes on patients."

She nodded. "Tucker?"

"Slight concussion. Some bruising. He'll be okay. He's lucky from what I heard from the EMTs. The truck's pretty much demolished."

"And the drunk driver?" she asked.

"Also lucky to be alive. He's here, too. Cops are with him."

"I should hope so. How could he drive drunk?"

"Not the first and sadly, not the last."

"Is Tucker ready to go home? I'll drive him."

"Not tonight. I want to keep him here overnight just to be sure. If all goes well, he can leave in the morning around ten. Do you want to spend a few minutes with him before we take him upstairs? We still need to get a bed ready."

Jenny nodded. The doctor led her down the hall and pulled a curtain back slightly to allow her to enter the cubicle. Tucker was lying on the exam table, eyes closed.

Jenny saw the bruising on the left side of his face, with a bandage covering a portion. He wasn't wearing a shirt and his left shoulder was beginning to show discoloration, as was the diagonal line across his chest from the seatbelt.

The doctor left and Jenny moved to the side of the table.

"Tucker?" she said slowly, reaching out to take his hand.

He slitted his eyes a bit and tried to smile. "Hey."

"Tal called me. I'm so sorry. The doctor said you'll be okay, though. How are you doing?"

"My head's killing me, but they gave me some pain meds," he closed his eyes and sighed softly. "I'm hoping they kick in soon."

"I'm sure they will."

She held his hand wishing there was something else she could do. But he'd received care and now it was up to time to heal the injuries.

"Can you call Mackay?" he asked suddenly sounding alert. "Tell him I'll be back tomorrow. Get him to send one of the men to get me. The sheriff said the truck's totaled."

His voice trailed away and Jenny could tell he was drifting off as a result of the pain medication.

"Yes, I'll call him and then I'll come pick you up tomorrow."

"You live too far away," he murmured, eyes still closed.

"That is a matter of opinion, I could say you live too far away."

He halfway smiled.

"There's a house on the ranch," he said slowly.

Was he drifting off to sleep?

"I thought it was for married cowboys," she said.

"If we lived there neither would be too far away."

Jenny held her breath. Was he aware of what he was saying? It almost sounded like he wanted them to live together.

Which was probably way off base.

"Do you think your boss would allow that?" she asked, humoring him.

She really wanted more clarification, but Tucker didn't appear very lucid.

He didn't respond.

"Tucker?"

No response. His breathing was deep and even. He'd fallen asleep.

Jenny stayed beside him until the nurses came with a gurney to take him to his room.

"You can go up with him if you want," one of the nurses said.

"No, it's late, and he's out for the count. I'll head for home."

Jenny gave Tucker's hand one last squeeze and leaned over brushing her lips against his cheek. "I'd love to share that house with you, Tucker Mason," she whispered.

As she left, she smiled at the nurses. "Take good care of him."

"We will."

12

Jenny and Val arrived at the hospital promptly at ten the next morning. She was anxious to see Tucker and make sure there'd been no surprise developments during the night.

She was directed to his room and when she arrived on the second floor she noticed his door was wide open. Stepping inside the room, she saw him fully dressed in the clothes he'd worn last night, blood stains visible on the shirt and his jacket. He stood by the window, looking out.

"You ready to go?" she asked.

He turned and smiled when he saw her.

"Ready."

He picked up some papers on the table beside the bed and walked over to her.

"Thanks for coming. You could have had Mackay send one of the men."

"I called him last night or rather early this morning I guess it was to let him know about the accident. He offered to come in himself, but I said I was closer and would be coming. He'll be there when you get home and you're not to work until a doctor gives you a total release."

"Naw, I'm fine."

"Headache gone?" she asked as they began walking down the hall.

"Mr. Mason, wait," the charge nurse called him from the desk.

He turned.

"We need to get you a wheel chair."

"I don't think so," he said. "Thanks for all your care, but I'm fine."

He took Jenny's arm gently and walked quickly to the elevator. Luckily the doors opened immediately and he wasted no time in stepping inside and closing the doors.

"It's standard hospital procedure," Jenny murmured.

She was amused at Tucker's determination not to wait for the wheelchair.

"Maybe, but I don't want to be pushed like a baby."

"Headache gone?"

"No, but it's not as bad as last night. And I feel stiff all over."

"You were lucky."

"Yeah, so I've been told. The other guy's more messed up."

"So no complications?"

"None, but the doctor said to take it easy for a few days. Nothing to jar my head. So no riding."

"Sensible precaution."

Once they were in Jenny's jeep and heading back toward Wildcat Creek, he looked at her.

"I appreciate the ride. Do you know where the ranch is?"

"No, only what you said before, about it's being on the

other side of town. You'll have to direct me. Tell me what you remember about last night."

"I was almost through town. The light at the corner of Third and Main just changed green and I was going through the intersection when a car slammed into my side of the truck, knocked me halfway down Third Street."

"Tal said it was a drunk driver."

"Yeah and I hope he throws the book at him."

"Me, too. I'm glad you weren't hurt more than you are."

"My truck's totaled, though. I liked that truck."

"You can get another one. There won't ever be another Tucker Mason."

He nodded. "I guess."

They drove in silence for a while.

"At least I get to see the house on the ranch," she said after a moment.

He looked at her sharply.

"What house?"

"The one you asked me to share with you," she replied in a teasing tone.

Did he remember saying that last night while doped up on medication?

She secretly hoped he'd issue the invitation again now that he wasn't doped up.

"I didn't say it out loud," he groaned, rubbing his hand over his face.

"So, you didn't mean it?" she teased, her heart racing.

He looked at her.

"Did you mean what you said before you left last night?" he returned.

It was Jenny's turn to look at him. Turning back to the road, she could feel heat rise in her cheeks.

"I thought you were asleep," she said.

"I thought I was dreaming. Did you mean it?" he persisted.

"And if I did?"

He gave a whoop and reached out to take her hand. "Pull over."

Her heart pounding, she checked for traffic and pulled off onto the shoulder of the road.

As soon as she put the jeep in park, Tucker leaned across and kissed her.

"I heard you last night and wanted to respond. But I was too far gone with the pain meds. So you'll share that house with me? If I can get the boss to let me have it? I love you, Jenny Schofield. I love every bit about you from your determination, to your sweetness, to your loyalty, to everything!"

"I love you too Tucker Mason," she said breathlessly, her eyes sparkling.

Val barked from the backseat.

"I come with baggage," she reminded him. "No telling when I'll freak out, as Sadie puts it."

"I think between Val and me we can manage anything you throw at us, right boy?"

Val barked again in affirmation.

Jenny laughed.

"I'm thinking parked on the side of the road isn't the best place for this," she said, giving him a quick kiss.

"You may be right, but it's important we get it all straight."

He took a deep breath.

"I want to spend the rest of my life with you. Marriage, kids the whole bit."

She smiled.

"Sounds doable," she said and kissed him again, her heart overflowing.

It was several minutes before she put the car in gear, pulling safely out on the highway.

"I called my mom this morning," Tuck said. "It turns out almost being killed in a car crash had me thinking about life and choices and the possibility of never seeing loved ones again. So I called."

"I'm hoping it went well?" she asked.

"Yeah. She was glad to hear from me. More than glad, I guess. She started crying."

He made a wry face.

"Well, what did you expect? She was probably beyond happy that her baby called her."

Tuck gave her a look and Jenny giggled. A big muscular cowboy like Tuck was hard to envision as a baby.

"Are you going to see them?" she asked.

"We talked about it." He was silent for a moment. "Want to go to Texas with me?"

Jenny threw him a glance, panic threatening. She took a deep breath. "Thanks for the invitation, but I don't even go see my own mom. Flying anywhere isn't something I feel I can do at this point."

The mere thought of being confined in a metal tube flying

through the air for hours almost had her melt down in the car.

"At least think about it."

"I will, but don't count on me," she said, concentrating on her driving and trying not to visualize the confined interior of a plane.

"I caught up on some of the news of my brothers. And an interesting tidbit—Trish and Aaron got divorced less than two years into their marriage."

"Sounds like that Trish isn't too good with relationships and how they should work. Or commitment," Jenny said somewhat sharply.

She didn't believe Tuck still cared for the woman, but she still hurt that he hurt.

When they reached Wildcat Creek, Tuck directed her through town and to the road that led to the Bar 7. Before long they arrived at the ranch. Following his instructions, Jenny drove to the bunkhouse and stopped.

"You start your new assignment tomorrow, right?" he said.

She nodded. "I'll be there at least a week. One of the grandmothers arrives next weekend. So if the baby's okay by then, I'll be finished."

"The doctor told me to take it easy, so if I get the time from Mackay, I thought I'd take the next few days and head for Texas. If you're sure you don't want to come with me. I can easily wait until the grandmother arrives."

"I'm sure I'm not going."

It made sense for her to avoid stressors, but for a moment, she felt disappointed. She wanted to spend more time with him right now. He said he loved her. She hardly had time to bask in his declaration before she had to deal with him taking off to the place where his first love lived.

Jenny sighed softly and smiled, though it took a lot of effort. He said his home was now in Wildcat Creek. But would Texas prove too alluring?

"Call me when you get there, so I know you arrived safely," she said.

She wouldn't try to change his mind. She was glad he reconnected with his family. She bet they missed him these last few years.

He cradled her head in his hands and kissed her. "I love you, Jenny."

She smiled and tried to keep from showing her sadness that he was leaving.

"I love you, too, Tuck. Come home soon."

13

Jenny arrived at the Perkins's home Monday morning to be there when Evie Perkins and her newborn daughter Annie arrived. The young husband had to go to work and was reluctant to leave even after Jenny assured him she had everything under control. She had the instructions from Evie's doctor and her pediatrician. Her duties would be more monitoring than anything else. If a crisis arose, Jenny was right on the spot.

Annie was adorable. She slept more than anything. She wasn't very fussy when she woke, but that could be because Jenny picked her up at the first sign she was awake. Changing and feeding her, she rocked the infant until she slipped back to sleep.

Evie primarily needed rest and was able to take long naps both morning and afternoon. She made an effort to spend time with her daughter when she was awake, but following doctor's orders, she slept whenever she felt tired.

Because Jim Perkins, the new father, had to leave early each morning and didn't return until almost time for dinner, Jenny had no free time during the day. She wanted to buy a mobile phone as Tuck had suggested, but so far had no chance to go shopping.

Once she had a little time, she'd dash out and buy one. Then she and Tuck could talk during her free time in the evenings.

The second evening she asked permission to use the Perkins' phone to call Tuck. She didn't know if he'd already left for Texas. Permission was granted and she hurried to call before it got too late only to discover she'd left the paper with his number written on it at her cabin.

"Blast it," she murmured, after dumping her purse on her bed and searching through everything.

"How could I not have brought that?" she asked Val.

The dog wagged his tail, his gaze focused on Jenny.

She looked up the Bar 7 and called there, discovering Tuck had already left for Texas.

"I told him he could recuperate as easily there as here and I wasn't letting him out on the range until his doctor said he was cleared," Bill Mackay told her.

Thanking the rancher, she hung up, wondering how Tuck's homecoming was going.

The tiny nagging reminder that Trish was there, and single, kept popping up at the most inopportune times.

He was over Trish. He'd moved on. He said he loved *her*, Jenny reminded herself even as her frustration with not being able to contact him rose.

Annie's grandmother was due to arrive late Sunday afternoon. Jenny expected to return home Monday morning if the doctor gave Evie and Annie a release.

Saturday morning, Jenny settled Annie for a morning nap, gave Jim instructions on what to do if the baby woke before she returned. She then headed to the phone store. She hoped to have time to dash home to get Tuck's phone number as well once she bought her new cell phone.

It was a hectic morning. There was a line at the store, then Jenny had to have the clerk show her how to operate the phone. It needed to be charged so she bought an automobile charger. She used the store's phone to check on how Jim was managing. When he sounded confident, she decided to dash home to get Tuck's number. The ride to and from the cabin should be enough to charge the battery so she could make a call.

It was mid-afternoon by the time she returned to the Perkins' home. She arrived to a crying baby, a crying mother, and a frantic father. In less than ten minutes Jenny dealt with everything, putting both Evie and Annie down for naps and suggesting Jim take a walk outside to get some time to himself. Though cold, it was a nice winter's day. He could use the diversion.

Once silence returned to the house, she phoned Tuck.

To her disappointment, the call went to voice mail.

"Hi Tuck. It's Jenny. I bought a cell phone like we talked about. I'm still at the Perkins' home in Coleville. But I'm probably heading for home Monday morning. Umm, call me. Unless I'm dealing with the baby or something, I should be able to talk."

She gave him her new phone number and then ended the call.

"He wasn't there," she told Val. "And with the way my luck's running this week, he'll call back when I'm feeding or changing Annie. Oh well, we'll just have to deal with that when the time comes."

Jenny began to get concerned when she prepared for bed and still hadn't heard back from Tuck. Was he so busy he couldn't call her back?

Or had returning home changed his mind about things?

Sunday morning when she had a moment Jenny called Sadie to see how the elderly woman was doing. Her former patient was as feisty as ever already talking about how soon she could return to church. Her friend MaryLou was planning to take her until she could drive again.

"And how's that cowboy of yours?" Sadie asked at one point.

"He's in Texas," Jenny said, trying to keep her voice even. She wanted to tell Sadie her wonderful news, but held back. Would the trip to Texas change his mind?

She really wanted Sadie to say something to help her not feel so uncertain about things. But if she didn't tell her about the offhand proposal, how would the older woman know to say the things that would make her feel better?

"He went to visit family I suppose. Didn't he ask you to go with him?" Sadie asked.

"Actually, he did. But I said no."

"Then that's on you. He obviously wanted to introduce you to his family."

Jenny hadn't considered that. They hadn't known each other for long, though she knew she loved him. And he'd said he loved her. She almost blurted it out his proposal to Sadie, but wanting to hug the secret close, she held back. Besides, what if he didn't return?

"I don't know about that," she said.

"From the way he looks at you, I'm sure that's what he wanted. Next time he asks, say yes."

Jenny agreed, smiling at Sadie's push for matchmaking. She'd be happy to go if she could get over her fear of being enclosed.

They chatted a few more minutes and Jenny gave Sadie her new phone number. She couldn't get service at her home, but would get it at most places she worked. She didn't want to lose touch with Sadie.

Next she called her friend Darcy. She hadn't talked with her in a week and wanted to give her friend the new phone number.

"Where have you been?" Darcy said as soon as she recognized Jenny's voice. "I've been calling you for days. Where are you?"

"On a job in Coleville. And I got a cell phone. So now I'm calling you from my job. What's up?"

"Julie Anne, eight pounds four ounces, born Monday. I can't believe my best friend didn't even know my baby's born."

"That's fabulous. Oh, I wish I'd known earlier! Tuck was right, I needed a cell phone. Now when I'm home you can call me on the land line or if I'm on a job not in the boonies of Wyoming, you can reach me on this phone. Tell me all about her. You're home already, right?"

Darcy told her about dashing to the hospital, how the baby was almost born before they got there and how delighted the whole family was to welcome a sweet baby girl.

For the first time ever, Jenny began to think about what

marriage would be like–settling down and having a baby of her own one of these days.

Could she master her PTSD in order to be a good mother?

She was doing well, so far, with all her nursing assignments. She delighted in working with little Annie. She was the first baby she'd worked with since training days and she loved every moment.

As if thinking of the baby woke her, Jenny suddenly heard her fussing on the monitor. She told Darcy she'd call again in a couple of days and be over to see Julie as soon as this assignment ended.

Dashing in to get the baby, she swiftly changed her and went to prepare a bottle. Jim and Evie were in the living room and she carried their daughter in to them.

It was late when Jenny checked her phone. She saw she had a message from Tuck; it had come when she'd been talking with Darcy.

He merely said he was returning her call.

She tried his number and again it went to voicemail. It was Sunday evening, where could he be? She disconnected without leaving any message. What could she say?

After the doctor's visit on Monday, both mother and child were declared doing well enough to dispense with a nurse at home. The grandmother was given instructions on things to watch for, and all the emergency numbers.

Happy for the new family, Jenny packed up her things and headed for home.

When she drew near the cabin, she saw a large black pickup truck sitting there. She hurried to pull into her normal spot and threw open the door, beating Val out of the jeep.

Tuck stood by the truck and started toward her as she ran to greet him. His open arms welcomed her when she threw herself into them. Val barked and danced around them.

"I'm so glad to see you!" she said, hugging him.

He picked her up and spun her around, kissing her, hugging her tightly. "I took a chance you'd be coming this morning as you said. I was just about to give up."

She gazed up into his dear eyes.

"I'm so happy to see you. I was afraid you'd be so glad to be in Texas you'd stay," she confessed shyly.

He put her back on the ground, brushed her hair away from her face and gazed into her eyes.

"No way, sweetheart. You're here, not there. Of course I came back. Plus, my job's here, not in Texas."

"I know, but your family's there, the ranch you grew up on."

She didn't say it, but she also thought *Trish was there.*

"I know and I was glad to see everyone. I have nieces and nephews I didn't know about. We caught up, talked late into the night every night. But it's not home anymore. This is home. Where you are is home."

He kissed her gently.

The words warmed her heart. Her worries of the last few days had been needless.

She studied the man she'd fallen in love with. She could picture the future, the two of them complimenting each other, completing each other, loving and supporting each other for all time. Happiness seeped into every bit of her like melting snow. She knew she'd love him all her days.

"Come in and tell me all about your visit," she invited, her arms still around his neck.

"In a second. This can't wait." He drew a small box from his jacket pocket and flicked it open.

"I want to do this right," he said, dropping to one knee.

"Jenny, I'll love you forever, will you marry me?"

Tears flooded her eyes and her heart raced.

"Yes, yes, I'd be so happy to be your wife."

He rose and slipped the ring on her finger, satisfied it fit perfectly.

"We need to seal the deal," he said gathering her into his arms again and kissing her.

Val lay down with a soft chuff, his eyes on the kissing couple. Was he thinking back to the day he rescued the cowboy? Slowly his tail began to wag.

—The End—

If you liked **Valentine's Cowboy Rescue**,
you'll love **Shelly and the Cowboy**,
book two in the Cowboys of Wildcat Creek series.

If you enjoyed **Valentine's Cowboy Rescue**,
please consider leaving a review.

More books by Barbara McMahon

Cowboys of Wildcat Creek
Valentine's Cowboy Rescue
Shelly and the Cowboy
Kristi's Cowboy Hero
Holly's Reluctant Cowboy
A Cowboy for Eliza

Sweet Reunion Romance Collection
Unexpected Reunion
Unpredictable Reunion
Unanticipated Reunion

The Talmadge Sisters
Letters to Caroline
Michelle's Marriage Deal
Trusting Abby

The Harts of Texas Series
Rebel Heart
Tangled Hearts
Reckless Heart

Cowboy Heroes Series
Blue Bells on the Hill
Cowboy's Bride
One Stubborn Cowboy
Crazy About a Cowboy
Never Doubt a Cowboy
Cowboy Marshal
Summer Cowboy
Second Chance Cowboy
Movie Star Cowboy

Tropical Escape Series
Island Rendezvous
Come into the Sun
Island Paradise

Tropical Escape Series
Island Rendezvous
Come into the Sun
Island Paradise

Rocky Point Series
Rocky Point Legacy
Rocky Point Reunion
Rocky Point Promise
Rocky Point Hero
Rocky Point Inn
Rocky Point Dawn

The Ultimate Billionaires
The Cynical Sheikh
Falling for the Sheikh
A Sheikh of Her Own
The Unforgettable Sheikh

Sweet Romance Stand-alone Collection
Because of You
Cowboy Charade
I'll Take Forever
Jared's Promise
Mail Order Bride
Not Really Married
Sweet Meant To Be
The Cowboy Comes Home
The Paper Marriage
Trusting Jake
The Banished Bride

A Sweet Clean Christmas Romance Collection
The Christmas Cop
The Cowboy's Special Christmas
A Soldier's Christmas
A Teaspoon of Mistletoe
The Christmas Locket
A Key West Christmas

www.ingramcontent.com/pod-product-compliance
Lightning Source LLC
Chambersburg PA
CBHW070038260626
47159CB00005B/2077